"I need to know that you'll remain invested in my sister's rescue. You, personally."

When Will would have interrupted, she put up a hand to stop him. "You're well respected in the police department and your name and title carry weight. I know this because my husband is connected in the court system, and he tells me things. Detective Reyes may be the better detective, but you're the one who can keep the search going for as long as it takes." She stared him straight in the eyes. "I need to know you won't stop looking for my sister...no matter what."

No matter what. The meaning of her request wasn't lost on Will. "We're a long way from that."

"Are we? In less than twenty-four hours, Thora's abductor threatened to end her life."

"The threat could be a bluff," Will said. "We're treating it as though it isn't—"

"Then say it." Thora's sister cut him off. "Tell me what I need to hear."

"I won't stop looking for her." *Ever.*

DIGGING
DEEPER

AMANDA STEVENS

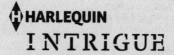

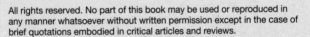

HARLEQUIN®
INTRIGUE™

ISBN-13: 978-1-335-59034-3

Digging Deeper

Copyright © 2023 by Marilyn Medlock Amann

For questions and comments about the quality of this book,
please contact us at CustomerService@Harlequin.com.

Harlequin Enterprises ULC
22 Adelaide St. West, 41st Floor
Toronto, Ontario M5H 4E3, Canada
www.Harlequin.com

Printed in U.S.A.

Amanda Stevens is an award-winning author of over fifty novels, including the modern gothic series The Graveyard Queen. Her books have been described as eerie and atmospheric and "a new take on the classic ghost story." Born and raised in the rural South, she now resides in Houston, Texas, where she enjoys binge-watching, bike riding and the occasional margarita.

Books by Amanda Stevens

Harlequin Intrigue

Pine Lake
Whispering Springs
Digging Deeper

A Procedural Crime Story

Little Girl Gone
John Doe Cold Case
Looks that Kill

An Echo Lake Novel

Without a Trace
A Desperate Search
Someone Is Watching

Twilight's Children

Criminal Behavior
Incriminating Evidence
Killer Investigation

Visit the Author Profile page at Harlequin.com.

CAST OF CHARACTERS

Thora Graham—Kidnapped and buried alive, the former FBI analyst tries to retain her sanity by conducting a methodical investigation into her own abduction.

Will Dresden—Racing against the clock, the new deputy chief of police desperately follows clues hidden inside a video and a series of taunting text messages.

The Weatherman—Incarcerated on death row, has he found a way to exact his revenge against the FBI analyst who caught him?

Professor Logan Neville—How far is he willing to go to eliminate his competition?

Addison March—An ambitious grad student who has wormed her way into Professor Neville's good graces...and his bed.

Baylee Fisher—A criminology student with ambitions—and secrets—of her own.

Elise Barrett—Will's ex-partner seems determined to prove she's the better detective.

Noah Asher—Has his obsession with the Weatherman turned him into a killer?

Chapter One

The wooden box was a tight fit, a perfect fit. If she stretched her toes and tipped back her head, she could just touch both ends. Her shoulders brushed against the sides, and she could only lift her hands a few inches above her chest. It was dark inside that box. Not the blackness of night, but a complete absence of light.

Thora Graham turned her head to the side and tried not to vomit. Slowly, she counted to ten as she struggled to control the nausea and the hysterical wail that was lodged in her throat. When she'd awakened earlier—minutes ago? Hours ago?—she'd lost control, screaming in terror as she tried to push open the lid of the container. In her frenzy, she'd expended too much oxygen too quickly and blacked out. Now she knew to be more careful.

Contorting her neck and body, she managed to place her mouth over a PVC pipe through which fresh air flowed. Another count of ten as she beat back a stronger wave of panic. *Think!* What did she know of her current predicament? Not much.

At some point during a rare evening out, she'd been drugged and placed in a wooden box the size of a coffin.

Was she underground?

Hysteria once again bubbled. She gulped more oxygen.

The air tube was a clue. She was being kept alive for a reason. That meant she had time to find a way out or, at the very least, figure out who had put her in here and why. FBI analysts were trained to search for obscure threads and anomalies, to fit all the pieces of a puzzle together. But she no longer worked for the feds. The Bureau's vast resources couldn't help her out of this jam. She had to rely on her wits and on the skill and resourcefulness of a man whose heart she'd once broken.

He'll come.

Will Dresden was a good man and, more important to her at that moment, a tenacious detective. He'd spent years running investigations before a promotion had tied him to a desk. Deputy Chief Dresden. She'd been back in Belfort, Texas—a small city near the Louisiana border—for nearly six months and his title still took her by surprise. She couldn't imagine him in an office. The paperwork alone would aggravate him. Fieldwork had always been his passion, but what did she really know about him these days, anyway?

She wondered if he had the same problem accepting *her* new moniker. Professor Thora Graham. Adjunct professor, to be precise, since she considered her position at the University of Southeast Texas—U-SET—to be temporary. From Quantico to a small regional school in one 'fell swoop. *How the mighty have fallen.* Never mind that it had been her choice to leave the Bureau. She'd seen the writing on the wall. The notation in her record would stymie future advancements. Maybe it was for the best. Maybe a change was all she needed to get her life back on track. But was that really something she needed to be worried about when she might only have hours to live?

Inhaling more air, she closed her eyes and pretended to feel a breeze across her face. It was hot inside the box. Nighttime temperatures were bad enough, but in the heat of the day, the container would become unbearable. Even with a supply of fresh air, she wouldn't last long. Dizziness and confusion would set in, accompanied by rapid heartbeat and shallow breathing. Her skin would turn red-hot and her muscles would weaken. She might experience seizures before she lost consciousness and fell into a coma. Then, death.

She shuddered and tried to turn her thoughts away from the inevitable. What time was it, anyway? How long had she been trapped? Her best guess was several hours, but it was hard to measure the passage of time since she'd been unconscious for much of her confinement. Still, she had clues. The effects of whatever drug she'd been given—Rohypnol most likely or possibly ketamine—were starting to wane and thirst wasn't yet a problem.

Closing her eyes, she tried to relax her cramped muscles as she directed her mind to the last thing she could remember. It was Friday night, and she'd been invited for drinks at a popular pub near the university to celebrate a colleague's birthday and the end of the summer session. Any number of excuses had flitted through her head when she'd been asked. She was tired. She had finals to grade. She needed to check in on her mother. Over the years, she'd become adept at bowing out gracefully, which was why her social life had been nonexistent since returning to her hometown. Despite having been born and raised in Belfort, she felt like a fish out of water. Most of her old friends were long gone or busy raising families and she'd never been that great at forging new relationships, even with the people she saw every day. Since the death of her husband five years ago, she'd sunk deeper into the seclusion of her work, obsessing over cases and becoming all too comfortable behind her computer screen. The social aspect of the classroom was a whole new world for her.

"Of course, you'll go," her sister had insisted as she'd fussed with Thora's hair. "A night out is just what the doctor ordered. You say you don't fit in here anymore. Well, what do you expect when you act as if you're just biding time? Don't bother denying it. We all see it. Even Mother. This is your chance to prove that you're not waiting for something better to come along. You're one of them. And like it or not, you're one of us, too. The prodigal daughter, as it were."

Prodigal daughter? Did Claire really think of Thora as wayward and repentant? She had regrets like everyone else, but her time in the FBI had hardly been misspent. She'd found success and purpose in her work, and before Michael's death, she'd been happy. Still, her sister's point was well taken. For however long she planned to stay in Belfort, she needed to make an effort.

The pub had been crowded and noisy. The cheery chaos had been off-putting at first, but Thora had forced a smile as she joined her group. Just her luck that her first social outing had to include her nemesis. She winced at the term. *Nemesis* was an overstatement, but she had little patience or regard for Logan Neville and his ego.

Ten years ago, the tenured professor had penned a true crime opus that had sat at the top of the best-seller list for over a year. His talk show appearances, along with his charm and charisma, had garnered an almost cult-like following, but without a successful sequel, his literary presence on the national stage had eventually faded. Locally, however, he was still something of a rock star, particularly in the Department of Criminal Justice and Criminology at U-SET. A classic big fish in a small pond, though his weekly podcasts had recently created ripples when he and a few of his star pupils had solved a cold case that had eluded local law enforcement for years.

Professor Neville's classes were always the first to fill up—or had been until Thora arrived on the scene. Her own credentials included the seven-year manhunt of a notorious serial killer named James Ellis Ridgeway. Dubbed the Weatherman because of his penchant for killing during inclement conditions, Ridgeway's hunting ground had spanned the I-10, from Alabama to New Mexico. The long gaps of dormancy and his cross-country killing sprees had kept him at large for nearly a decade, but Thora was nothing if not persistent. Once she'd been assigned to the case, her dogged research and in-depth analysis had eventually helped guide the FBI and local law enforcement to Ridgeway's modest brick home on the outskirts of Mobile, Alabama.

Her real-world experience with the National Center for the Analysis of Violent Crime, and in particular, her time with the Behavioral Analysis Unit, made her an irresistible draw to the more serious and ambitious students in her department. For whatever reason, Professor Neville seemed to take her popularity as a personal affront. But was he threatened enough by her expertise to drug, kidnap and bury her alive?

Methodically, Thora worked her way back from

their brief interaction at the pub to every other meeting with Logan Neville that she could recall. Conducting a mental investigation clue by clue, thread by thread, kept her from clawing at the lid of the coffin until her fingers bled. It kept her sane.

Take another breath and concentrate.

Using every ounce of her willpower, she forced her mind's eye to linger on each person seated around the two tables that had been shoved together to accommodate their large party. People had come and gone from the group all night. Some left temporarily to play darts or shoot pool, while others like Professor Neville mingled with a few students that had gathered at the bar. Thora couldn't help but notice how blatantly he flirted with one of the young women. She'd heard rumors of his notorious affairs. Every year, he picked a favorite grad student to mentor, and more often than not, the relationship turned sexual. His most recent acolyte was his TA. Addison March was smart, beautiful and sophisticated for her age, the type of ambitious young woman who would be drawn to an older, urbane academic like Logan Neville.

There'd been some kind of ruckus at the bar earlier that night. Thora strained to recall the details. Angry words between Addison and another student named Baylee Fisher had erupted into an ugly shoving match that Professor Neville managed to break up. Thora had been surprised to see Baylee at the pub, let alone involved in a physical confrontation. From what she'd observed in the classroom and around campus, Baylee was a shy introvert who mostly kept to herself. She was smart and driven, but in every other way the complete opposite of Addison. How the former had ended up in the latter's orbit was anyone's guess. That Neville was somehow in the middle was hardly a shock.

Thora wondered if her wine had been spiked during those awkward moments when everyone's attention had been riveted on the clashing students. Unlikely. She would have felt the effects long before her departure a few hours later. Besides, she was always on guard in public places. She knew better than to leave a drink unattended, even among friends. She hadn't left the table until she'd finished her first glass of wine, and if the second glass had been laced with a knockout drug, it may have occurred at the bar.

Which brought her to the stranger. He'd been seated on a stool with his back to the room, but she'd noticed his reflection in the mirror behind the shelves of bottles and glasses. He was tall, attractive, well-dressed. And he'd been staring at her. As their gazes met in the mirror, he slowly rotated the barstool so that they were facing one another across the crowded pub. The back of Thora's neck had prickled in excitement. Or was it a warning? There'd been something unnervingly familiar about his half smile, about the hard, knowing glint in his eyes as he lifted his drink in salute.

Her pulse accelerated at the memory. Hysteria choked her again. She sought the air tube and counted to ten.

Stay calm. Don't let fear trip you up. What else do you remember?

A little while after the confrontation between the students, Will Dresden had come in with an attractive blonde. Thora didn't want to dwell on that particular aspect of the evening because the smile he'd flashed at the woman and the protective way he'd taken her hand as they navigated the crowd had jolted Thora in a way she would never have imagined. *Did you really think he'd wait for you forever? You left him, remember? You went off to Virginia and got married.*

Thirteen years was a long time to carry a torch. Of course he'd moved on. These days, he was nothing more than an old acquaintance. A stranger, really. They had nothing in common except ancient history.

He'll come.

No matter their past or any lingering bad blood, Will was a professional. He'd leave no stone unturned once he knew she was missing, but how long before anyone realized she'd been taken? Claire and her husband were driving to Houston for a wedding the following day and wouldn't return until late. Thora had a brunch date with her mother on Sunday, but could she hang on for that long? What did her abductor have in store for her? How long would she be allowed access to the air tube?

She pounded on the lid. "Can anyone hear me? What do you want? Just tell me what you want!"

Placing her ear to the pipe, she listened intently for a sound that would give away her location. Nothing came to her. No traffic, no barking dogs, nothing but the echo of her heartbeat inside the box. For all she knew, she was miles from town, miles from anywhere. How would anyone ever find her?

He'll come. Please, God, let him come.

Chapter Two

On the rare Saturday morning when Will Dresden didn't have to go to the station for a meeting or to catch up on paperwork, he liked to sleep in. Today, however, one of the neighbors had decided to cut his grass at what seemed like the crack of dawn and Will had awakened with a groan and a string of oaths. It was only a matter of time before some jerk fired up a leaf blower.

You're just cranky because you know you should be out there doing the same thing. Why he'd ever thought home ownership a good idea was beyond him at this ungodly hour. Maintenance, repairs, yard work. The chores never ended, and on a morning like this, he longed for his old apartment.

He plopped a pillow over his head and tried to drift off again, but then—typically—the phone rang. There'd been a time when he might have been able to ignore the annoying ringtone, but his promotion had come with added responsibilities. As one of two deputy chiefs with the Belfort

Police Department, he supervised the Criminal Investigations Division, which included Major, Special and Property Crimes units, Vice, Narcotics, Domestic Violence, Missing Persons and CSU. Which meant he was basically always on call. He grabbed his cell without checking the screen and hit the accept button.

"This better be good," he barked, expecting to hear a muttered apology from one of his rookie detectives. Too late, he realized the caller might well be *his* superior, a former Marine who brooked no disrespect or insubordination from his underlings. The Belfort Police Department was small compared to that of the neighboring city of Houston, but in the last ten years, drug and human trafficking in the area had exploded. Despite the challenges of a limited budget, Chief Burnett remained committed to running a tight ship.

"Hello?" The tentative voice was female and sounded faintly familiar. "I'm calling for Will Dresden."

He expelled a breath of relief and adjusted his tone. "This is Dresden," he said politely.

There was a nervous hesitation before she said, "I'm sorry to call so early on a Saturday morning, Will. I hope I'm not disturbing you. Your brother said I could probably reach you at home—"

"Who is this?"

Another pause. "It's Maddie Graham. We used to be next-door neighbors. Your mother and I were best friends before she remarried and moved away."

And your daughter and I used to be lovers.

A thousand images swirled in Will's head as he swung his legs over the side of the bed and ran a hand through his clipped hair. "She still speaks of you fondly," he said. "What can I do for you, Mrs. Graham?"

"I'm not sure. You'll probably think I'm over-reacting…" She trailed away and started again. "I'm calling about Thora."

His pulse quickened despite his best efforts. "What about her?"

"You've heard she moved home a few months ago? She's an adjunct professor at U-SET. She taught the spring semester and now she's just finishing up the summer session."

"Yes, I heard she was back." He rose and walked to the window to glance out. "You must be happy about that. She's been gone a long time." Thirteen years to be exact. He rubbed the scruff on his face as he idly tracked the offensive mower and thought, *what an odd conversation for so early in the morning.* It seemed a lifetime ago that his family had lived next door to the Grahams. A life-time ago since he and Thora—

"—didn't know who else to call."

The tension in Maddie Graham's voice snapped Will back to the present. He scowled out the window as a beam of early morning sunlight caught him in the face. "What's going on?"

"She went out last night. I haven't been able to reach her since."

He refrained from pointing out the obvious, that Thora was a grown woman who had been trained in self-defense at the FBI Academy. A night out was hardly cause for alarm. "I'm sure there's nothing to worry about," he said. "I saw her at a pub on Second Street last night. She was with a group of friends."

He heard her draw a sharp breath. "You saw her? Did you talk to her?"

"As I said, she was with friends. I didn't want to intrude."

"But…she seemed okay?"

"I only caught a glimpse of her, but she seemed fine." He let his mind drift back for a moment. Despite a growing population, Belfort was still a small enough community that he'd recognized several of the people seated around the table. But his attention had lingered only on Thora. She wore those thirteen years well. Maturity suited her, as did the soft waves of dark hair that framed her face. Strange to think that she was a widow at thirty-five. He could feel sympathy even as a more troubling emotion stirred beneath the surface. Jealousy? Resentment for a dead man after all this time?

Probably a good thing he'd been on a date. Otherwise, he might have done something he would have later regretted. Like striking up a conversation or offering to buy her a drink. That ship had sailed a long time ago and he'd learned the hard way that when it came to old relationships, the past was best left buried.

"Did you see her leave the pub?" Maddie asked anxiously.

"No, I left first. It was still early. Probably around nine thirty or so. You want to tell me why you're so upset? She probably got home late and turned off her phone so she could sleep in."

"She wouldn't do that," Maddie insisted. "I've been having some health issues lately. She'd want to make sure that I could reach her."

"I'm sorry to hear that," he murmured.

"It's been an ongoing problem for a while now. Thora moved back to Belfort to help out. She wanted to take some of the pressure off her sister now that Claire's pregnant. And I think there may have been some personal reasons for the move as well. She'd never say anything, of course, because she wouldn't want to worry me. But a mother can tell when something is wrong—" She broke off as if realizing she might have strayed too far from the original intent of her phone call. And maybe her daughter's old boyfriend wasn't the person in whom she should confide. "I don't mean to ramble on like this."

"No, I get it," Will said. "You're worried."

"Yes." Her voice caught and she fell silent for a moment while she gathered her poise. "I'm sorry. It's just such a relief to say it out loud. I didn't want to upset Claire this morning when we talked so I tried not to let on how scared I was. But I can't shake the feeling that something bad has happened. I was a cop's wife for a long time. I learned early on to trust my intuition. Your mother would know what I mean by that. The two of us used to commiserate when one of our husbands was late checking in."

"I remember."

"Rationally, I know it's too early to be so upset, let alone to file an official report. Thora is a grown woman and I saw her less than twenty-four hours ago. The police would think I'm a foolish old woman with too much time on her hands. That's why I'm calling you, Will. I realize I'm putting you in an awkward position, but you were once like family to us and I can't help thinking that if something truly is wrong, then time may be of the essence."

"I'll be happy to help in any way I can," he said, keeping his voice low-key. "When was the last time you spoke to her?"

"Yesterday around six. She stopped by the house on her way to meet friends. She didn't want to go out last night, but her sister and I encouraged her. Browbeat might be a better word. You have no idea how deeply I regret that now." Her voice trembled with emotion.

"Take your time," he said.

Another few seconds went by before she said softly, "Claire and I thought it would do her good to get out more. Make some new friends. She's become so reclusive since she lost Michael."

"That was the last time you heard from her?" he asked, ignoring the reference to Thora's dead husband.

"Yes. She said she'd call when she got home last night if it wasn't too late. When I didn't hear from her, I took it as a sign that she'd had a good time. But when I couldn't reach her this morning, I started to worry so I called Claire. She and her husband drove by Thora's place on their way out of town and then they went by the pub. They found her car in the parking lot, but no sign of Thora anywhere. That's when I called your brother to get your number. I heard about your promotion. I was hoping you could pull some strings. The longer we go without hearing from her..."

"I'll do what I can," Will assured her. "My advice at the moment is to try and stay calm. It's too early to jump to any conclusions. Is it possible she had too much to drink and called a cab or ride-sharing service? That could explain why her vehicle is still at the pub."

"Absolutely not. She never has more than a

glass or two of wine, but even if she did, she'd still answer the door and her phone."

Maybe she went home with someone.

Will thought of the man at the bar eyeing Thora in the mirror. He'd seemed so fixated that Will had sidled up to the bar and bumped against him, pretending to be jostled by the crowd in order to check him out more closely. The man had shrugged at Will's apology and turned away, but not before Will had caught the quick flare of annoyance in the stranger's eyes.

Aloud he said, "Did Claire say whether or not the vehicle was locked? Did she notice anything out of place? Any dents or scratches in the paint?" *Any blood stains on the door handle?*

Maddie gasped. "Do you think Thora could have been in an accident?"

"Right now, I'm just asking questions. As I said, there's no reason to assume the worst. Thora is a trained professional. She knows how to take care of herself. Let's assume for a moment that she did have too much to drink. If she's nursing a hangover, she might not have heard her phone or the doorbell. It's even possible she spent the night with a friend." When Maddie tried to protest, he said quickly, "If it'll put your mind at ease, I'll take a run over to her place and check things out for myself. In the meantime, sit tight and try not to worry. I'll call you when I know something."

"Don't you need her address?" Maddie asked.

"Uh, yeah. Let me put it in my phone." No need to, though. News traveled fast in Belfort, Texas. He knew where Thora lived. Her complex was only a few miles from his neighborhood. He'd taken the long way home once just so he could drive by the gated entrance. He wasn't sure why. He told himself it was just idle curiosity.

"You'll need the gate code."

"Thanks."

Fifteen minutes later, he was showered, dressed and ringing Thora's doorbell. It was still early and the complex was quiet except for the swish of sprinklers that watered the tropical landscaping. Thora's front stoop was recessed into the brick facade, affording privacy from three angles. When no one answered, he tramped through one of the flower beds to glance inside her front window. The blinds were open, but the glass was tinted to keep out the blistering rays of the Texas sun. He could see little more than shadows inside. He rang the bell one last time before returning to his car.

His next stop was the pub. He wheeled into the parking lot and pulled up next to Thora's dark blue Volvo. He got out and checked the locked doors, then circled the car. No dents, no scratches, no sign of foul play, but the abandoned vehicle lifted the hair at the back of his neck. He trailed his gaze over the building, noting the location of the security cameras. Maybe something had been caught on video.

Maybe there was nothing to catch. A former FBI analyst had had a few drinks with colleagues and then left her car in the parking lot because she'd had the good sense not to get behind the wheel. She wasn't answering her door because she'd spent the night with a friend. No reason as of yet to think anything untoward had happened except for that unsettling irritation at his nape.

He circled the car a second time, then lowered himself to the pavement and checked underneath the vehicle. Nothing...no, wait. What was that? He thought at first the dull gleam of metal was a pull tab from a soft drink can, but he flattened himself against the ground and reached for it anyway.

Then he rose, clutching a key ring with a single latchkey attached. The key could have been there for months or even years, dragged from someone's purse or pocket and forgotten. But the brass wasn't weathered or tarnished and the fact that he'd found the key beneath Thora's abandoned car triggered yet another alarm.

He pocketed his discovery, then rounded Thora's vehicle a third time, peering through the windows and examining the door handles for blood stains. Satisfied that he hadn't missed anything, he drove back to her townhouse and tried the key. The lock *clicked* open and the door swung inward with an ominous squeak.

Hovering on the threshold, he trailed his gaze through the narrow foyer as he called out her

name. "Thora? You home? It's Will Dresden."
He entered slowly. "Thora Graham?"

A sensor had chirped when he opened the door,
but the system had been deactivated. The question was, by Thora or someone else?

Don't jump to conclusions.

She'd only been missing for one night and part
of a morning. For all he knew, she wasn't missing
at all, but had simply failed to check in with her
mother. She might walk through the front door at
any moment and catch him standing in the middle
of her foyer. He could only imagine the look on
her face. Best case scenario, they'd have a good
chuckle over the awkwardness of their first meeting. But Will wasn't laughing now. Like it or not,
he was also starting to have a bad feeling about
her absence.

He walked from the foyer into the living room
and then on through to the kitchen, taking care
not to touch anything. The townhouse was well-
appointed and spotless, yet an ominous feeling of
abandonment had already descended.

Every room was as clean and tidy as the last.
In the kitchen, the dishwasher had been emptied.
Upstairs, the bed was neatly made. No discarded
clothes on the closet floor, no damp towels in the
bathroom. How disciplined one must be to keep a
place so meticulous, he mused. And where were
her personal mementoes, the keepsakes from her
travels and the awards and accolades accumulated

from a successful career? Where were the photos of her late husband?

The only trace of Thora that lingered was the faint scent of lavender in the bathroom. The subtle fragrance brought back another round of memories. He'd always loved the smell of her hair. He turned abruptly and went back downstairs, stepping into the small rear courtyard for a breath of fresh air as he called Maddie.

She answered on the first ring. "Thora?"

"It's Will Dresden."

"Will." Her worry and disappointment were palpable. "Please tell me you've found her. Is she okay?"

"I'm sorry. I don't know anything yet, but I'm at her place now. Either she didn't come home last night or she left the house early this morning. Her bed's made and the coffee maker washed. Might she have caught a ride to her office to grade papers or something?"

"Why wouldn't she have gone back to the pub for her car? And anyway, she'd still have her phone with her," Maddie reasoned.

"True."

She paused. "How did you get into her townhouse? Claire said both the front and back doors were locked."

"I found a key underneath the Volvo." No use keeping the truth from her. The poor woman was already imagining the worst. He remembered that

Thora's mother had always been a worrier, but in this instance, he was beginning to think she had every right.

"Underneath her car?" she repeated in horror. "How did it get there, do you suppose?"

"She must have dropped it as she was leaving the pub."

"Then she never made it home last night," Maddie whispered.

Unfortunately, that was also Will's conclusion.

"I was right to be worried, wasn't I? Something's happened to her."

Will gentled his tone. "We don't know anything yet, but I do need to ask you a few questions. I'd like to come by your house if that's okay. Maybe it would be a good idea to ask Claire to come over and wait with you."

"She and her husband canceled their plans as soon as they found Thora's car. They're on their way here now. We'll do whatever we can to help. Answer as many questions as you need to ask. But Will…tell me the truth. You're worried, too, aren't you? I can hear it in your voice."

"Not worried. Concerned, is all. I'm on my way over. Hopefully, you'll have heard from her by the time I get there."

"Will?"

"Yes?"

"Thank you."

"I haven't done anything yet."

"You're taking me seriously. That means everything to me."

Her gratitude humbled him. "You don't need to thank me for doing my job. Just try to stay calm, okay? I'll see you in a few minutes."

He walked back to his car and got in, scowling through the windshield as he swept his gaze over the buildings and grounds. The meandering pathways and shadowy courtyards seemed portentous somehow, as if evil had slipped through the gated entrance while no one had been looking. Maddie Graham's dread was contagious. Will felt tense, restless, like he needed to be out combing the streets for Thora. He had to remind himself that there wasn't yet sufficient cause for alarm, but the circumstances were concerning. Her pattern of behavior had been broken. And why wasn't she answering her damn phone?

He thought again of the man at the bar and his unwavering focus on Thora. That wasn't so unusual in and of itself and certainly no crime. Thora was a beautiful woman. She drew attention even in a crowd. Still, the intensity of the man's gaze had bothered Will. He wished now that he'd struck up a conversation with the stranger. Maybe a few pointed queries from a cop would have been enough to send the guy on his way. Instead, Will had gone back to his table, finished his drink and left the pub with his date. Maybe if they'd stayed even ten minutes longer, he could have prevented…what? *What do you think happened to her?*

A car pulled into the adjoining space. A woman in white trousers and a yellow top climbed out and headed up the walkway toward Thora's building. Will got out of his vehicle and called to her. "Excuse me, ma'am! May I have a word?"

She turned with a start, ducking her head to peer at him over the frames of her stylish sunglasses. "Are you talking to me?"

"Yes. Do you live in this building?" He held up his badge and ID as he approached.

Her expression turned anxious as she glanced at his credentials. "I live in 4B," she said. "Has something happened?"

"Do you know the woman in 4A?" He nodded toward Thora's door.

"The teacher? We've met. I wouldn't say I know her exactly." The neighbor shoved her sunglasses to the top of her head as she gave him a nervous scrutiny. "What's this about, anyway? What did she do?"

"She didn't do anything. I just need to speak with her. When was the last time you saw her?"

She shrugged. "I really couldn't say. I don't keep track of my neighbors' comings and goings."

"Try to remember," he pressed. "It could be important."

She adjusted the strap of her shoulder bag as she glanced past Will to the covered commons area just inside the entrance. "If I had to guess, I'd say it was probably at the mailboxes."

"Can you be more specific?"

"Not really. Like I said, I don't keep track." She gave him another assessment. "I do find all these questions a bit strange, though. For someone who hasn't done anything wrong, she sure has a lot of people looking for her."

Will's voice sharpened. "What do you mean?"

"I didn't think much of it until you showed up just now, but another guy came by a couple days ago. That was on Thursday, I think." She seemed to consider the time frame and nodded. "Must have been around six or so. I remember because I was getting home from my yoga class. He stopped me on the walkway just like you did. Claimed to be an old friend. He said Thora had asked him to come by, but she wasn't answering the door or her phone. He wanted to know what time she usually got home from work."

"What did you tell him?"

"Nothing." Her gazed hardened. "Unlike you, he didn't have a badge, and I wasn't born yesterday. I figured there was a reason she didn't want to talk to him."

"Did he give you a name?"

"I didn't ask for one."

"Can you describe him?"

"Tall, slim, late thirties or early forties. His hair was longish and kind of unkempt, like he couldn't be bothered to run a comb through it. Other than that, he was nicely dressed and attractive if you didn't look too closely. But there was something about him that didn't add up."

"How so?"

She smiled. "I work for a lawyer. I know a thing or two about suspicious behavior."

"Go on."

"I couldn't shake the feeling that he'd been looking for a key under the doormat when I walked up. He tried to make it seem as though he dropped his phone, but I didn't buy it. He was up to no good. Smooth and handsome on the surface, but the eyes will always give a guy like him away." She cocked her head as she searched Will's face.

"You didn't think about calling the police?"

"And tell them what exactly? I couldn't prove he was looking for her key, could I? Besides, he would have been long gone before you guys got here."

She had a point. "Did you happen to see his vehicle when he left?"

"No. But I did wonder how he got through the gate."

"Maybe he followed another car through," Will suggested.

"Maybe. Or maybe he was telling the truth and she gave him the code. I doubt it, though."

Will didn't think so, either. He wished he'd snapped a shot of the guy at the bar last night to see if the neighbor recognized him. He handed her a card. "If you see him again, I'd appreciate a call."

He thanked her for her time and went back to his vehicle. A text message pinged as he backed out of the parking space. After braking, he checked the display. A video from an unknown number appeared on the screen. He pulled his car back in and pressed play.

The black-and-white footage had been shot in a confined space using a fiber-optic camera, not unlike the kind plumbers used to determine the source of a clogged pipe. Will couldn't make sense of the scene at first, but realization dawned as a familiar voice called out, "Can anyone hear me? What do you want? Just tell me what you want!"

She appeared to be lying on her back in a rectangular container. The lens had been situated above her so that he could only see her profile and upper torso as she pounded frantically on the lid of the box. Then she dropped her hands to her sides as she placed her mouth against what he could only guess was an air tube. After a few moments, she fell back against the bottom of the container and closed her eyes.

The video ended and a moment later, a second one appeared on his phone. The new footage had been shot during the day, probably early that morning given the angle of the shadows and the softness of the light. The camera zoomed out to reveal a wide-angle view of a densely wooded area that seemed to extend for miles. Then the lens focused back on a single pipe protruding about a foot out of the ground.

Just then, another text pinged.

They say you're a clever investigator, Will Dresden. A smart lawman whose talents and intellect are wasted in a Podunk town like Belfort, Texas. I say they're wrong. Dead wrong.

How much skill is required to round up a few tweakers and gangbangers every week?

Will texted back:

Who is this?

The replay came instantly.

Think of me as your Moriarty (look him up!).

The mockery wasn't lost on Will. He scowled at the screen as he thumbed his message.

Is she alive?

Yes, but for how long depends on you.

What do you want?

Several seconds went by until Will began to worry that the conversation had ended. And then:

I want to see how you measure up against a worthy opponent. You've probably deduced from the video that your precious Thora is at this very moment buried six feet under. You've got twenty-four hours to find her before the air tube is removed. Good luck, Deputy Chief Dresden, and may the best detective win.

Chapter Three

Thora awakened with a start. For a moment she thought she must still be dreaming. Darkness pressed in from all sides and the heavy weight of claustrophobia threatened to crush her. She lifted her hands expecting—hoping—to find nothing but air above her. Instead, her palms pressed up against a wooden barrier. The box. The nightmare came rushing back. She was trapped inside a coffin-sized container with only a PVC tube to supply air. No food, no water, no means of escape. For all she knew, she was deep underground, buried in the middle of nowhere.

Hysteria welled in her chest as panic clawed at her throat. Her impulse was to scream for as long and as loud as she could until someone heard her cries and came to her rescue. Instead, she counted to ten, then twenty, then fifty as she tried to slow her racing heart. Her head pounded and her throat burned. She needed water. She needed air.

She sought the tube and drew in measured breaths. How long had she been asleep? *How* had she been able to sleep? Was she still under the influence of whatever drug had been slipped into her drink? Or was she drawing poison into her lungs at that very moment, causing lethargy and then unconsciousness?

So many questions swirled in her throbbing head, none of which could be answered in her agitated state. She concentrated on clearing the cobwebs from her brain. As the fog began to lift, her breathing slowed and the pain in her head subsided. She flexed her cramped muscles for relief. It was hot inside the box. Perspiration drenched her hair and clothing and her skin felt feverish. She would grow weaker with every second of captivity, but if she preserved her energy, if she refrained from trying to fight her way out of the container, she might get through this. Or she might only prolong the inevitable.

What if no one had even missed her yet? Her mother and sister would try to reach her at some point, but by the time they panicked enough to call the police, it might be too late. If no one reported her missing, how would Will know to look for her? She still wanted desperately to believe that he would come, but wishful thinking could only keep her sane for so long. Already she could feel the tentacles of despair coiling around her fragile resolve.

Shake it off. Shake it off! You'll get through this.

One minute at a time, one hour at a time, one day at a time…

He'll come.

She had to cling to that fleeting hope because it was all she had left. Will was an excellent detective, as good as they came. She'd kept up with his career over the years. She knew of the offers from big-city police departments, even from the FBI. He could have gone anywhere, pursued any specialty, but he'd stayed in Belfort because he felt it was the right thing to do, initially for his family and then later for his community. He'd stayed while Thora had fled.

Strange how much he'd been on her mind lately, even before the abduction. She'd found herself hoping to catch glimpses of him on the rare occasions when she happened to be downtown near police headquarters. She'd been dreaming about him before she awakened just now. Visions from their past mingled with the stolen glances from yesterday evening. She'd tried not to be obvious when he came into the pub, but it was hard not stare after so many years. He looked good. Older. More confident and maybe a tad jaded. More guarded, too, she'd noticed, though that might only have been projection. But the dark hair was the same, thick with a slight wave. And from what she'd been able to tell from across a crowded and dimly lit bar, the same intensity still smoldered in his blue eyes. What those eyes had once done to her.

Guilt prickled at her even after all this time, even under extraordinary circumstances. Michael had been gone for half a decade. There were days when their short marriage seemed surreal, like a hazy, half-forgotten dream, but her memories of Will Dresden were sometimes so vivid that their time together might only have been yesterday. Maybe that wasn't so surprising. She'd known Michael Fleming for less than two years in total, but she and Will Dresden had grown up next door to one another, had attended prom together, graduated high school and gone to college together. They'd been inseparable for so long that back then Thora couldn't have imagined her life without him—until she could.

Seeing him in the pub had brought back so many of those old memories. So many of those old feelings, too, if she dared to be honest with herself. But dwelling on what might have been never did anyone any good. Especially not her. Not now. Not here in the box when her next moment was an uncertainty.

Shuddering in the stifling heat, she closed her eyes and tried to center herself. Panic was only a hair's breadth away, but if she succumbed to the terror, she might never find a way out. If she started to scream, she might never stop. So she did the only thing she could think to do in her current situation: she resumed her investigation.

With the passage of time, bits and pieces of her

night out had started to come back to her. She forced herself back into the noisy chaos of the pub as she mentally explored the room. A little while after Will and his companion left, she'd decided to call it a night. The timing was a coincidence… or so she told herself. Their exit had nothing to do with her leaving. She'd simply had enough. The loud music and constant chatter had started to wear on her nerves.

Plus, the eye contact with the stranger at the bar had left her unsettled, though if pressed for a reason, she couldn't explain why. Maybe she'd been out of the game for too long, but his attention seemed more derisive than flirtatious. She couldn't imagine why. She was certain they'd never met, yet his slow smile had triggered her defenses. She didn't know him, but his sardonic salute seemed to suggest that he knew her. Had their paths crossed since she'd moved back to Belfort or had he followed her here from Virginia?

An unnerving thought, but a long shot. Her job with the FBI had required almost no contact with the general public and even less face-time with the criminals she'd studied and tracked. She never ran investigations or made arrests. The bulk of her workday had been spent staring at a computer screen, so chances were slim that she'd attracted the attention of a stalker or someone who harbored enough of a grudge to shadow her all the way down to Texas. Still, she couldn't discount the possibility. She'd been a target two years ago. Maybe her tormentor had resurfaced, but kidnapping would be a dramatic escalation from anonymous phone calls and text messages. Even the break-in at her apartment seemed innocuous compared to being trapped inside a box.

She'd been certain at the time that the harassment was somehow connected to the Weatherman case. The incidents had occurred within weeks of James Ellis Ridgeway's conviction and incarceration. Thora's role in his takedown had been leaked to a reporter. After her name had appeared online, she'd begun receiving dropped calls in the middle of the night, followed by a series of taunting and vaguely threatening text messages. On several occasions, she'd spotted someone in the park across the street watching her building. The stalking had culminated with the break-in at her apartment and then, just like that, it was over. The police detective assigned to her case concluded that she'd been the target of a malicious prankster. Nothing had been taken from her home and no overt threats had been made. His suggestion was to put the episode behind her.

Thora had managed to do exactly that. Compartmentalizing various aspects of her life had become second nature to her. She'd retreated back into her low-profile existence, burying herself once again in her work. Eventually, the seven years she'd devoted to the capture of James Ellis

Ridgeway grew less significant to her career as more monsters came along for her to track. The Weatherman, like all the others, became nothing more than a case study, a subject to be dissected and analyzed and then filed away.

Two years had gone by without further incident, but the job had started to take a toll. Thora's decision to move back home had had nothing to do with a stalker. The phone calls and text messages were long behind her, and she had no reason to think her current predicament was in any way connected to that brief episode. Yet she couldn't get the stranger at the bar out of her head. She couldn't stop picturing his taunting smile and knowing stare.

Taking another gulp of air, she kept her focus in the pub, letting her mind's eye wander through the room. At some point after Will and his date exited, she'd left her second glass of wine unfinished and said good-night to her colleagues. She knew there had been significant conversations and observations between her arrival and departure that she could later examine, but right now, she wanted to concentrate on the moments leading up to the abduction.

She remembered feeling a little light-headed when she rose from the table. She wasn't by any means intoxicated, but she couldn't deny a strange unsteadiness as she made her way through the crowd. By the time she left the building, nausea bubbled in her stomach as the parking lot started to spin. Stumbling toward her car, she fumbled for her phone to call Claire. Something was wrong, but if she could just make it to her vehicle and lock the doors until help came...

The bright lights had come out of nowhere, catching her directly in the face. Blinded and disoriented, she threw up a hand to shield her eyes. The sudden motion initiated the vertigo. She staggered back as the asphalt tilted beneath her feet. A car door slammed and then someone grabbed her arm, holding her upright.

"Don't fight it."

The voice in her ear sounded strange, distorted, electronic. A million miles away.

"Who are...? What do you...?" Her own speech came out slurred, almost unrecognizable. "What did...?"

"It'll be a lot easier if you just let go."

Thora had a vague recollection of being shoved inside a vehicle. She remembered the sound of the engine, the flicker of passing car lights and then nothing. The next thing she recalled was waking up in the box.

Thankfully, the nausea and dizziness were finally subsiding, which meant several hours must have passed since she'd been drugged. Maybe it was morning. Maybe her mother had already tried to call her. She would want to hear about Thora's night out. When she couldn't reach her, what then?

Would she call Claire? The police? How much time would she let go by before she sounded the alarm?

Putting her ear to the PVC pipe, she strained to detect a noise from the outside world. Anything would have been welcome.

Nothing like that came to her, but there was a sound on the other end of the air tube. Faint taps. She listened for a moment, her pulse leaping in excitement before she put her mouth to the opening.

She called up into the pipe, "Hello? Is someone out there? Can you hear me? Can you please help me?"

The drumming grew louder. She wondered if she'd imagined the sound. A strange pattern emerged, rhythmic and hypnotic. Tap, tap… pause…tap, tap. Tap, tap…pause…tap, tap.

"I don't understand. What do you want from me?"

Tap, tap…pause…tap, tap. Tap, tap…pause… tap, tap.

She put her fist to the lid of the box and repeated the sequence.

A few drops of water landed against her face. Was it raining?

Almost euphoric by the feel of moisture against her dry lips, she let the water trickle into her mouth and down her parched throat. *Careful. Don't get strangled.* When she'd had enough, she tapped out the sequence on the air tube. The dribble stopped.

"Hello? Are you still there? Please, what do you want? Just tell me what you want."

Her pleas seemingly fell on deaf ears.

She banged her fists against the lid of the container. "Let me out of here! Please! I haven't seen your face! I don't know who you are! Nothing will happen if you just let me go!"

When no response came back to her, she pounded even harder. "Let me out of here! Do you hear me! *Let me out of here!* You can't keep me here. You can't do this!"

She was seriously in danger of losing control, but she didn't care at that moment. She kept right on screaming and pounding until she grew hoarse and her bruised hands fell helplessly to her sides. "Please," she sobbed. "Please let me out."

After a moment, the rhythmic drumming came again. She placed her lips to the tube. When no water trickled out, she repeated the sequence and rasped into the tube, "Water. Please."

A few drops dribbled down the pipe. She lapped them up and then let her head fall back against the bottom of the container. "Thank you."

More drumming. She realized now the sound was a command. She wouldn't be given what she wanted until she answered in kind. She tapped out the sequence and waited. Instead of water, something cool and metallic slid down the tube and fell against her cheek. She groped in the dark until she had the object in her hand. Running her fingers along a chain, she found a circular charm. Even in the pitch blackness of the box, she knew the medallion was the one Michael had worn for good luck, a gift from the grandfather who had raised him. The keepsake had been tucked away in a jewelry box since the day her husband's personal effects had been returned to her.

Whoever put her in the box had been in her house, gone through her things and taken Michael's good luck charm for a reason. That chain had been around his neck the day he died. The medallion had lain against his chest the moment his heart had stopped beating. No other possession, including her wedding ring, would have had the same emotional impact. Somehow the kidnapper had known that. Delivering a gut punch when she was at her most vulnerable was a deliberately diabolical act.

She clutched the medallion to her breast. It would have been so easy in that moment to give up and let fear and despair take control. But she wouldn't. She couldn't. Not until she knew who was on the other end of the air tube. Not until she knew *why*.

She pounded fiercely on the lid and called up once again, "Who are you? What do you want?"

Nothing came back to her. No drumming, no

trickling water, nothing. The silence in the box became unbearably heavy.

Whoever had been on the other end of the pipe was gone, leaving Thora alone to brood in the dark confines of her prison.

Chapter Four

After leaving Thora's townhouse, Will drove straight to police headquarters to activate the necessary protocols for a kidnapping victim in imminent danger. He called Maddie en route to alert her of a new development, but he didn't go into specifics, and he kept the conversation short because he didn't want to break the news of Thora's abduction over the phone. Back at the station, he briefed his team before sending someone to the Graham home to meet with the family. He stayed behind to orchestrate the dozens of details that went into a citywide search. The situation wasn't ideal, but his title greased wheels and every second counted when a twenty-four-hour-deadline loomed over their heads.

By the time he finally pulled to the curb in front of Maddie's house, the Tech Unit had already scoured his phone and begun the painstaking task of analyzing the video. In the meantime, the Crime Scene Unit had processed Thora's townhouse and car and delivered sealed bags of trace evidence to the lab. More than a dozen officers had been dispatched to search the immediate area around the pub while every other available personnel tracked down the people that had been with Thora the previous evening. Law enforcement agencies within a hundred-mile radius had been alerted and a call had gone out to the FBI field office in Houston.

Will glanced at the clock on his phone as he got out of the vehicle. He'd received the videos and text messages just before nine that morning. The time was now closing in on noon. Twenty-one hours before Thora's air tube would be removed. How long could she last after that? So much would depend on her frame of mind and whether she could hold it together enough to conserve her strength and oxygen. That was asking a lot, even of a trained professional. He tried to put himself in her place…trapped in a box with barely enough room to raise her hands above her chest. Buried underground with no idea if anyone even knew she was missing.

He felt sick to his stomach when he thought of what she must be going through, but he couldn't afford to get sidetracked. Each and every unit in his division had an integral part to play in the search and he was the one who had to make sure the operation ran like a well-tuned engine. It was imperative that he stay focused and unemotional.

Thora's life might well depend on a split-second decision.

Maddie's son-in-law answered the door. Will knew the man only slightly by reputation. Jared Hartley was a partner in a big downtown law firm. Highly successful if the late-model X6 in the driveway was any indication. The two men shook hands and then Will followed the attorney across the narrow foyer and down into a sunken living room.

He took in the area with a single glance. Nothing much had changed since he'd last been there. The white slip-covered furniture looked the same, as did the framed photographs of Thora and Claire on the walls and the overkill of porcelain knick-knacks in the built-ins. Maddie and Claire sat side by side on the sofa. Detective Angel Reyes balanced his notebook on his knee as he faced them across the coffee table. Mother and daughter jumped to their feet when Will entered.

Maddie took an imploring step toward him. "Will—"

He headed her off before she could get her hopes up. "We don't know anything yet, but it's early. We're not even three hours into the search. We've mobilized the entire police force and have requested support from the FBI. I know it's hard not to worry, but we're doing everything we can to find her."

Maddie's shoulders drooped despondently. "I

don't even know how to process what's happened. Detective Reyes told us about the videos. Claire wouldn't let me watch them..." She clutched her daughter's arm. "What kind of person could do something so cruel to another human being?" She gazed up at Will, eyes pleading for answers.

He'd been asking himself the same question all morning. In the course of his career, he'd witnessed a lot of disturbing things, but video footage of a woman buried alive had to be one of the most twisted. The impact was even more devastating because he knew the victim. "The thing to remember is that she's alive, she's strong and she has an air supply. She'll be able to hang on until we find her."

"How are you going to do that?" Maddie wrung her hands in distress. "I know you'll do what you can, but she could be anywhere. It would take weeks if not months to search all the wooded areas around Belfort. Not to mention the swamps." She closed her eyes and swayed on her feet. "When I think about what she must be going through... I just don't know if I can stand it."

"We have a lot of smart and dedicated people going through those videos frame by frame, pixel by pixel," Will said. "We're searching her car, her home, the area around the pub. We'll find something. We always do."

Claire wrapped an arm around Maddie's frail shoulders and held on tight. "Come sit down,

Mom. And please, please try to stay calm. You know what the doctor said about your heart."

Maddie let her daughter lead her back to the sofa. "Nothing matters but Thora. I don't care what happens to me. I just want my daughter back."

"Well, I care," Claire insisted. "I'm worried about Thora, too, but it won't do her any good if you make yourself sick."

Will exchanged a glance with Reyes and nodded, signaling that the older detective should continue the interview. Meanwhile, Will stepped back so that he could observe the entirety of the room. Instead of being at his wife's side, Jared Hartley had retreated into the dining room. Will could see him through the wide casement opening that separated the two spaces. He was on his phone, but every now and then he'd glance up, as if one of the detective's questions had caught his attention.

Ignoring the attorney, Will looked through the dining room into the kitchen where he could see a portion of the backyard through the large window over the sink. He could even glimpse the roof of the old tree house that their dads had built when the families were neighbors. It was sad to think that the tree house had outlasted both of those tough men. Will's dad had gone first—killed in the line of duty—and then Thora's several years later from pancreatic cancer.

When Will had first learned about his dad, all

he could think was that he needed to get home as fast as he could to take care of his mother and younger brother. But later on, when the arrangements had been made and all the neighbors and fellow officers had departed, he'd gone outside and climbed up into that tree house to be alone with his grief. After a while, Thora had slipped through the hedge and followed him up. She'd known exactly where to find him that night. Somehow she'd always known.

Now it was his turn to find her. She was trapped in a box, buried only God and her kidnapper knew where. The task seemed overwhelming if not impossible. Maddie was right. Belfort was surrounded by hundreds of acres of dense forest and swampland. It would take a miracle to pinpoint Thora's location with nothing marking the site but a PVC pipe protruding a foot from the ground. *Like looking for a needle in a haystack.* Will had to trust that clues would be found in the video or that the lab would discover a print, a hair, a fiber—*something* from her car or townhouse that would help identify her abductor.

Rationally, he knew everything that could be done was being done, yet it took every ounce of his willpower to fight off a terrible feeling of inevitability, especially when he observed Maddie's haggard face. No matter how old the child, a mother's need to protect never waned.

He went back over the video in his head. Had he

missed something? Had he overlooked a subtle but vital piece of information that only he could decipher? The one clue that would lead him to Thora?

They say you're a clever investigator, Will Dresden. A smart lawman whose talents and intellect are wasted in a Podunk town like Belfort, Texas. I say they're wrong. Dead wrong.

A wave of anger washed over him, but he quickly stifled the emotion because he knew those taunting messages were meant to rile him up and throw him off balance. Make him second-guess his decisions. He forced a cool head as he went back over in his mind every line of the text. The sender had referred to Thora by name. *Your precious Thora.* Whoever had taken her knew their history—or wanted him to think so—but that hardly narrowed the field. Could be anybody. Someone Will had arrested. A former classmate or neighbor. Someone who carried an old grudge. Someone who likely regarded themselves as the smartest person in the room.

He caught Claire's eye. She gave him an enigmatic look before she stood and collected empty cups from the coffee table. A few minutes later, she returned with a tray of clean cups and a fresh pot of coffee. She served her mother and Detective Reyes first, offered a cup to her husband, which he declined, and then brought one over to Will. The outside temperature had already soared to the nineties and humidity hovered around sixty percent. It was way too hot in the middle of the day for a steaming drink, but he accepted the cup and murmured a thank-you.

"Can I talk to you for a minute?" She nodded toward the foyer. "Out there. In private."

"Sure." He followed her into the narrow entrance, glancing through the sidelights on either side of the front door to check the peaceful street.

The light streaming in through the narrow windows caught the diamond on Claire's finger as she tucked back her hair. The stone was square cut and just slightly smaller than ostentatious.

For a moment, she seemed unsure what to do with herself. She splayed her hands protectively across her still flat belly as she glanced over her shoulder into the living room. When she turned back to Will, her expression seemed almost blank except for a glint of anger—or was it fear?—in her brown eyes.

In that moment, she looked very much like her sister. So much so that Will was taken aback. Same dark, glossy hair. Same soulful eyes. Personality-wise, the sisters had always been polar opposites. The Thora he'd known could remain calm and collected in almost any situation while Claire, he suspected, still had a temper and a flair for the dramatic.

Her uncharacteristic silence seemed somehow portentous. He tilted his head as he gazed at her across the narrow expanse of the foyer. "You okay?"

The innocuous question snapped her out of her stupor. Her mouth thinned as she glared up at him. "I just learned that my sister has been kidnapped and buried alive so, no, Will. I'm not okay. I'm far from okay."

"I know."

"God, it's like a nightmare. I keep telling myself it can't be real, but it is. I saw the videos." She closed her eyes on a shudder. "You know what keeps running through my mind? All those years Thora spent with the FBI working cases that involved the worst kind of criminals. Finally, she gave all that up to come back to the one place where she should have been safe, and she ends up in the clutches of a human monster." Her voice shook with emotion as her gaze pinned Will with relentless intensity. "How could something like this happen in Belfort? How could you let it happen in our town on your watch?"

He did nothing to try to counter her rage. People reacted differently to fear and grief. Sometimes a person under stress or in crisis needed someone to blame. If Claire had chosen him to be the scapegoat, so be it. He could take it.

"We'll find her," he said.

Her chin shot up. "Is that a promise?"

He sighed and set his cup on a nearby table. "There are never any guarantees in a situation like this, but we're doing everything in our power to find her and bring her home safely. I can promise you that."

"Well, I'm sorry. That's just not good enough." Despite her anger, she managed to keep her voice low so that no one in the other room could overhear her tirade. "You've already let my mother down once today. You'll forgive me if I'm reluctant to take your promises to heart."

He kept his tone gentle. "What are you talking about, Claire? How did I let her down?"

"She called you for help this morning. She called *you*. You should have been the one to tell her about Thora instead of sending a stranger to her door to deliver the worst kind of news a mother can hear. She's always held you in the highest regard. You were once like a son to her. I would have thought after everything our families have been through together, you would have shown her that kindness."

So that was the root of her wrath. Or at least a convenient excuse. In truth, her anger probably had very little to do with him and everything to do with her own feelings of guilt and helplessness. He understood those emotions only too well.

"When your mom called this morning, she told me she had a feeling that time was of the essence." He glanced through the opening into the living room where Maddie sat with clasped hands and bowed head. "Turns out, she was right. Once I received those videos, a lot of wheels had to be set in motion as quickly as possible. I couldn't spare even a second. I didn't want to tell her over the phone or risk having her hear the news from someone else, so I sent Detective Reyes. He may be a stranger to you, but I've known him for years. He and I were partners for a time. He's one of the best investigators I've ever worked with, and I'd trust him with my life. That's why he's here."

"Is he better than you?" The way Claire challenged him made him think of the taunting tone of the text messages.

He answered without hesitation. "In this situation, he is unquestionably the better detective. He spent ten years in El Paso investigating cartel kidnappings. He has more experience working abductions than anyone in the department."

Claire seemed only slightly mollified. "Well, I hope and pray you're right. But for Mom's sake, I still need some assurances from you."

He suppressed an impatient sigh. "What kind of assurances?"

"I need to know that you'll remain invested in my sister's rescue. You, personally." When he would have interrupted, she put up a hand to stop him. "You're well-respected in the police department and your name and title carry weight. I know this because my husband is connected, and he tells me things. Detective Reyes may be the better detective, but you're the one who can keep the search going for as long as it takes." She stared him straight in the eyes. "I need to know you won't stop looking for my sister...no matter what."

No matter what. The meaning of her request wasn't lost on Will. "We're a long way from that, Claire."

"Are we? In less than twenty-four hours, Thora's air tube will be removed."

"The threat could be a bluff," Will said. "We're treating it as though it isn't."

"Then say it. Tell me what I need to hear."

"I won't stop looking for her." *Ever.*

Something in his voice seemed to convince Claire of his honesty. She nodded. "Thank you. I know I'm being difficult, but I couldn't bear the thought—" Tears filled her eyes and spilled over as if the gravity of her own request seemed to hit her. Will reached in his pocket for a handkerchief. He'd learned early on in his career that a clean linen handkerchief was sometimes more effective than a loaded weapon.

"Don't give up on her," he said.

She accepted the handkerchief and dabbed her eyes. "I'm not. But you know better than I the reality of the situation. I have to be mentally prepared so that if and when the time comes, I can be strong for my mother. She'll need me as she's never needed me before. It would be a comfort to know that you'll be there for her, too, Will."

"Of course, I will."

She handed the handkerchief back to him. "That's that, then." She straightened her shoulders and her chin came up once more, a stance he knew only too well from all those years with Thora. "I want to focus on the search now."

"What is it you want to know?"

"You mentioned earlier that you have people studying the videos and going through my sister's car and home, but is anyone actually out there looking for her? Has a search party been formed? I have nothing against Detective Reyes, but if he's as good as you say he is, shouldn't he be out there instead of in here wasting time with an endless stream of questions?"

"He's doing his job. The more questions he asks, the greater the chance that something will come back to you," Will explained. "Even the smallest detail could be important. Until we have a concrete lead on Thora's location, the best way to find her is to find the person who took her."

"Seems to me the best way to find the person who took her is to look for someone with a grudge against you." Her stare was stone-cold. "I read those text messages, Will. The tone was derisive and superior and the kidnapper referred to my sister as, your precious Thora. Whoever took her has to be someone who knows you and is familiar with your history."

"We haven't overlooked that possibility, but the list of possible suspects is long considering my years in law enforcement. We're in the process of scouring arrest records, flagging threats, tracking down inmates recently released from jail or prison. All that takes time."

"What about someone with a more personal grudge?"

He searched her features. "Why do I get the feeling you already have someone in mind?"

"Elise Barrett," she blurted.

He absorbed the shock, then said, "You're serious."

She scowled up at him. "Why do you find it so hard to believe? Because she's a cop or because she's a woman? Or because you were once engaged to her?"

He returned her scowl. "I don't know where you got that idea. Elise and I went out for a while. We were never engaged."

"Oh, really? Because she tells a different story. She called it an unofficial understanding. She said at the last minute you couldn't commit because you still had feelings for my sister."

There might have been more truth to that claim than Will wanted to admit. However, in all the months that he and Elise Barrett had been together, the subject of marriage never once came up. Where she'd gotten the notion of an understanding, official or otherwise, he couldn't imagine. He'd always been open about where he stood in the relationship, which was why when the time came to end things, he'd gone for a clean break. He'd always thought Elise felt the same way.

Maybe she had. Maybe Claire's interpretation was skewed by her current frame of mind.

"I didn't realize you and Elise were such good friends," he said.

Claire shrugged. "We aren't. Which is why I was so surprised when she cornered me at a party awhile back. She'd had too much to drink—way too much—and decided to unload her grievances. It was an illuminating conversation." Her gaze darkened. "That woman has a serious chip on her shoulder where you're concerned, Will. She said after you dumped her, she was forced out of the Criminal Investigations Division while you ended up with a promotion. Is that true?"

Will felt stunned by the revelation and more than a little angry. "She wasn't forced out. She asked to be transferred to Internal Affairs."

Claire gave him a tight, almost pitying smile. "Again, not how she tells it. Did you know that she and Thora had some kind of friendly rivalry back in college? Although now I have to wonder how friendly it actually was. This is going to sound truly bizarre, but I think *she* thinks Thora's career with the FBI should have been hers."

"She said that?"

"Not in so many words, but that's the impression I got. She never talked about Thora to you?"

"Not really. I never knew they were anything more than acquaintances."

"I think there are a lot of things you don't know about Elise Barrett," Claire said. "Are you going to send someone to talk to her or should I go confront her myself?"

"No, don't do that. You need to keep your distance. Let me handle this," Will said. "The best way you can help is to stay put and look after your mother. Earlier she mentioned something I've been wondering about. She said she had a feeling that Thora had reasons other than being close to family for moving back here. Do you have any idea what she meant?"

Claire shook her head. "No, but I wouldn't read too much into it. Mom is a worrier. She's always getting bad feelings about something. Sometimes her intuition pans out and sometimes it doesn't."

"You don't know of any problems or confrontations that Thora may have had at work or in her personal life?"

"She keeps things pretty close to her chest. I would never have known about all that business with the Weatherman if she hadn't let something slip. Then I badgered her into telling me the rest."

Will was instantly on alert. "What business?"

"It turned out to be nothing, but a few weeks after James Ellis Ridgeway was sent to prison, Thora started getting anonymous phone calls and text messages…" She trailed off. "You do know who Ridgeway is, don't you?"

"Every law enforcement agency along I-10 knows who James Ellis Ridgeway is."

"Okay, well, Thora worked that case for seven years. She's the one who connected his kills to weather patterns. She's the one who first suggested that something traumatic occurred in his childhood to make him equally repelled and fascinated by storms. Turns out, his mother used to lock him in a storm cellar for days at a time. No food, no water, no bathroom. Anyway, after his conviction, Thora's name appeared in an online article that went viral. The write-up wasn't very flattering. The reporter made her sound like an obsessed loner. Soon after the article was published, she started getting threatening phone calls and text messages."

"Threatening in what way?"

"Things like, *You're lucky the sun is shining today.* Or, *Be careful. There's a storm brewing tonight.* Nothing overt, but the underlying intimidation was clear. She came home one day to find that her apartment had been broken into, but nothing was taken. Nothing that she missed, anyway. After the break-in, the phone calls and texts stopped. She changed her number and the locks on her door and went about her business as if nothing had happened."

"She never heard from this person again?"

"Not that I know of. The cops chalked it up to a 'malicious prankster.'" She air-quoted the term before glancing over her shoulder. "We never told Mom. I would appreciate it if you didn't say anything. She doesn't need another thing to worry about right now."

"I won't mention it if I don't have to." Will removed a piece of paper from his pocket and unfolded it. "Take a look at this." He handed the computer-generated rendering of the stranger he'd seen at the bar the night before to Claire. "Do you recognize this man?"

She studied the image for a long moment. "I don't think so. Who is he?"

"He was seen in the pub last night at the same time Thora was there. Her neighbor said a man matching his general description came by her townhouse last Thursday looking for her. He claimed to be an old friend. He said they were supposed to meet but he hadn't been able to reach her by phone and she wasn't answering the door. Did Thora mention anything about a friend coming to town?"

"No. She never said a word. She's extremely private but I think she would have told me about a visitor." Claire glanced up from the rendering. "Do you think this man had something to do with her abduction?"

Before Will could answer, Jared Hartley came up behind his wife. He studied the image over her shoulder, then reached around and took the paper from her hand. "Who's this supposed to be?"

"Right now, he's a person we'd like to have a conversation with," Will said.

"He was seen in the pub last night the same time Thora was there," Claire explained as she turned to her husband. "You don't recognize him, do you?"

"No, but it's hard to say definitively from this drawing. He could be any one of a dozen guys you'd see in a bar on any given night."

"We're circulating the image in Thora's neighborhood and around campus. Maybe we'll get lucky and someone can give us a description of his vehicle. Or better yet, a license plate number." When Hartley tried to return the image, Will said, "Keep it. Study it. You never know when something may come back to you."

Hartley folded the paper and tossed it on the entrance table beside Will's abandoned coffee cup. "I'm sure I don't need to remind you of the ticking clock that's hanging over your head. A crime of this magnitude can make or break a reputation." He slipped his arm around Claire's shoulders. "I hope for my wife's sake, and for her sister's, that you're as good as they say you are, Dresden. The whole town will be watching."

Chapter Five

Will elected not to call Elise Barrett to request an interview but instead drove straight to her place after he left Maddie Graham's house. His decision was twofold. He wanted to keep the meeting casual while also catching her off guard. A spontaneous reaction could often be telling.

He still considered the possibility of her involvement in Thora's kidnapping slim at best. He'd known the woman for years. They'd gone through the police academy together and had worked side by side in the Criminal Investigations Division before her transfer to Internal Affairs. During their time as a couple, he'd never had anything but respect for the way she conducted herself personally and professionally. She had a wild streak. He wouldn't deny that, but she had her limits. His trip across town to see her was probably a huge waste of time, but he couldn't take the chance that Claire's instincts might prove right. What if he didn't know Elise as well as he thought?

She lived on the far east side in a little two-bedroom bungalow she'd inherited from her grandmother. The neighborhood had been working class until college students and starving artists discovered the affordable housing. With their arrival, the streets had taken on a distinctly bohemian air. The changing vibe hadn't bothered Elise as it had some of her neighbors. She'd wholeheartedly embraced the colorful murals and overabundance of yard art.

The scent from the roses that spilled over the neighbor's fence bombarded him as he climbed the porch steps and knocked on Elise's door. When she didn't answer, he rapped harder. Hearing signs of life inside, he tried a third time and waited.

She answered the door belting a silk robe around her waist. Judging by her damp hair and glistening skin, he'd gotten her out of the shower. She looked momentarily startled to see him and none too happy.

"What are you doing here?" Her gaze flicked past him to the street. "You're about the last person I expected to find at my door on a Saturday morning."

"It's the afternoon," he felt compelled to point out.

"Barely." She coiled her hair around her fingers and fashioned a bun at her nape. "What do you want?"

"I need to talk to you. It won't take long. Can I come in?"

She observed him through the screen. "This isn't a good time. Can you come back in an hour? Or better yet, call me later and we can meet somewhere for a drink."

"This isn't a social visit and it can't wait. I wouldn't be here if it wasn't important."

She glanced over her shoulder, then unlatched the screen door and stepped on to the porch. Will could have sworn he saw a shadow move inside before she pulled the wooden door closed.

"Well?" She leaned back against the door frame. "You wanted to talk, so talk."

Something about her attitude caught *him* off guard. He wasn't quite sure why he felt so on edge all of a sudden. Elise's expression remained one of mild annoyance, but her eyes seemed to guard a darker emotion. He couldn't help noticing that she'd checked the street a second time when she stepped outside. Was she expecting someone? Or was she worried he might recognize a car parked at the curb? And why would she care if he did?

He tried to gauge her reaction without overtly scrutinizing her features. "I need to ask you a question and I'm hoping you won't take it personally."

She folded her arms. "Which pretty much guarantees that I will but do go on. What's the question?"

No easy way to ask so he went for the direct

approach. "Where were you last evening between the hours of eight and eleven?"

"I shouldn't take that personally?" Despite the note of sarcasm, she didn't look particularly surprised or offended, just curious. "What's this about, Will?"

"Answer my question first and then we'll talk."

"Tell me what this is about and then I'll answer your question."

He started to counter but his attention was momentarily diverted by a twitching curtain at an open window. Maybe the breeze had stirred the panel, but he had a feeling someone stood on the other side listening in on their conversation. He shifted his focus back to Elise. "Did I interrupt something?"

"Yes, you got me out of the shower." She tucked back a strand of damp hair as she moved away from the entrance, forcing him to turn away from the open window and that twitching curtain. She plopped down on the low concrete wall that encased the shady porch and leaned back on her hands as she gazed up at him.

Outwardly, she seemed relaxed if still a bit peeved, but instinct told him she wasn't as calm as she'd have him believe. There was a reason for his uneasiness. He'd picked up on a worrisome vibe.

"I think I know why you're here," she said. "Is this about Thora Graham?"

He scowled down at her. "How do you know about that?"

"Last I checked, I'm still a member of the Belfort PD. You mobilize the entire police force on a Saturday morning, word gets out." Her expression turned serious. "Is she alive?"

An image of Thora lying flat on her back in that buried box flashed through Will's head, sending a cold chill down his spine. *Can anyone hear me?*

I heard you and I'm trying to find you. Just hold on.

He struggled to keep his tone and demeanor impassive. "We've every reason to believe she's alive." But for how much longer? He resisted the temptation to check his watch.

Elise shivered. "I can't imagine what she must be going through. It's surreal when you think about it. Here we are on my porch enjoying a nice breeze while at this very moment, she's out there somewhere, buried in a box in the middle of nowhere. Nothing but her own thoughts to keep her centered. And her poor family. They must already be worried sick."

"I was just with them," he said, still in a careful tone. "They're holding up as well as can be expected."

"And you?"

That was a loaded question. He refused to glance away from her probing stare. "I'm worried."

She gave me a pitying look. "The things one

human being is willing to do to another just keep getting sicker. Remember little Danny Hagan? The nine-year-old boy who disappeared in broad daylight while walking home from school? We were first-year detectives when he went missing. It killed me that we couldn't find him."

"That was a tough case," Will agreed.

"A decade later, still no trace. The world is a very dark place."

"Sometimes it can be."

"Cops see the worst of it. The first responders. I don't miss that part of the job. It's a particularly heavy burden when the victim is a child, or in this case, someone you know. I'd like to ask about leads, but I'm sure you're unable to share details of the investigation at the moment."

"No, I can't, but your intel seems pretty sound so far."

"Even an IA investigator has friends." She swung her legs up to the wall and hugged her knees. For a moment, she seemed mesmerized by a potted fern stirring in the breeze. Will glanced around. She'd always been into gardening. Terracotta planters crowded the small porch, and her front yard was like a jungle. He could still smell the neighbor's roses. The sticky scent reminded him of a funeral.

"I'm going to need an answer to my question," he said.

She glanced up at him, her expression still solemn save for a spark of defiance in her blue eyes. "Isn't it rhetorical?"

"Why would you think that?"

"I assume the reason you're here is because you already know that I was at Molly's Pub last night. You were there, too. And Thora. I also assume you're tracking down anyone you can think of who might have seen or heard anything out of the ordinary. Sorry to say, I didn't."

He said nothing for a moment. Then, in a quiet voice, "You were at Molly's last night?"

She looked surprised. "You didn't see me come in?"

He shook his head slowly.

"I guess that makes sense. The place was packed and you were otherwise occupied. New girlfriend?"

"A friend."

Something hard gleamed in her eyes. "Let's just back up for a minute. If you didn't see me, then why—" She broke off as realization seemed to dawn. "You really did come here to find out my whereabouts last night."

"That's what I said."

"Are you trying to tell me I'm a *suspect*?"

"I never said—"

Before he could finish his thought, she jumped to her feet. "That's the most ridiculous thing I've ever heard! What possible motive could I have for kidnapping the poor woman and burying her alive? For God's sake, Will. You know me. Do you really think I'm capable of something that evil?"

"I never said anything of the sort."

"This is *unbelievable*." In her agitation, the belt of her robe loosened and the silk lapels gaped, revealing an angry red scratch across her collarbone.

"Elise, what happened to your neck?"

Her hand flew to her throat as if she'd forgotten about the wound. "The hazard of trimming rose bushes. But you know that. You've seen scratches on me before. You used to berate me for not wearing gloves." She shoved up the sleeves of the robe so that he could see several grazes on her arms. "Now that I'm a suspect, maybe you'd like to subject me to an imprint analysis, just to make sure it was thorns and not fingernails that got me."

He ran a hand through his hair as he said wearily, "I never said you were a suspect because you're not."

"That's the implication. Why else would you be here?"

"You said it yourself. We're tracking down a lot of people and asking a lot of questions. Time is not on our side. We can't afford to overlook any possibility no matter how remote. When there's a ticking clock, we have to cast a wide net."

She wasn't buying it. "Why me, specifically? Your explanation made sense before I realized you had no idea that I was at the pub last night. You knew I wasn't a witness so why single me out? Why waste precious time driving all the way over here when you could be out there looking for Thora?" Her mouth tightened. "Someone pointed a finger at me, didn't they? I still have friends in the department, but I've also made enemies. Who sent you here, Will?"

She was starting to work up a good head of steam. Will couldn't say that he blamed her, but the last thing he needed was to lose control of the situation. He kept his voice purposely calm, almost dismissive as he explained his predicament. "It's not like that. I'm only here because certain information was brought to my attention and either I came knocking on your door or someone else would. This seemed the best option. Just a casual chat between old friends."

Her eyebrows soared at that. "What's the information? If someone is making accusations, overt or otherwise, I have a right to know the identity of my accuser. You tell me *exactly* why you're here or this conversation is about to get very loud and extremely unpleasant."

Will glanced across the street where a neighbor watering her yard with a garden hose stood watching them. He lowered his voice as he turned away from her prying eyes. "Thora's sister told me about a discussion the two of you had a while back."

"Claire Hartley is the reason you're here?" She

looked utterly bewildered. "Wait. Are you talking about what happened at that party last winter?"

"Claire said you two had an illuminating conversation."

Elise winced. "More like the equivalent of a drunk dial." She seemed genuinely embarrassed about the incident. He could see a faint blush beneath her freckles. "Talk about making a mountain out of a molehill. Everything said that night was meaningless. I got hammered and shot my mouth off. End of story."

"We've all been there," he muttered.

Her chin came up. "And yet you were perfectly willing to come over here and interrogate me based on a one-sided account of a drunken conversation."

"This is hardly an interrogation," he said. "I agree, the information Claire provided is thin, but there's another component you may not be aware of. We've reason to believe the person who took Thora has a grudge against me. Claire seems to think you've still got a chip on your shoulder from our breakup. Do you?"

She looked as if she wanted to deny the contention, then shrugged. "You know how it is. You get strung along for months then dumped. Tends to leave a bad taste."

Will canted his head. "And here I thought we had a mutual parting of the ways."

"You would think that."

"What's that supposed to mean?"

"Nothing." She moved back to the edge of the porch and leaned a shoulder against a post. "You never answered *my* question. Do you think I'm capable of something so heinous as kidnapping a woman and burying her alive?"

"Of course I don't. I'm just trying to do my job, Elise."

"Then I'll make it easy for you. Since you've already pissed me off, you may as well ask any other questions you have that I shouldn't take personally."

The sarcasm was thick with that one. The whole conversation was starting to leave a bad taste for Will. "What time did you arrive at the pub last night?"

"Eight thirty, nine. I ordered a beer at the bar and went to the backroom to shoot some pool. The tables were full and there was a line. You know me. I've never been one to watch and wait my turn, so I left early and went straight home. Alone."

He resisted the urge to glance over his shoulder at that open window. "What time was this?"

"Ten-ish."

"You said you saw Thora at the pub?"

"I caught a glimpse of someone I thought was her. She was seated at a table with a large group of people I didn't know."

"You didn't talk to her?"

She sighed and crossed her arms. "Why would I talk to her? I haven't seen her since college, and we were little more than acquaintances back then. We had a couple of classes together and that's it. I doubt she even remembers me."

Will studied her expression, intrigued by the flicker of conflicting emotions she couldn't quite conceal. "Claire seems to think you and Thora were rivals."

"Rivals for what? You? Don't flatter yourself." She sounded even more irritated. "Besides, everyone on that campus knew the two of you were joined at the hip. No one in their right mind would have tried to come between that."

"Let's go back to last night."

She smirked. "Why? Is the conversation making you uncomfortable? Par for the course. You've always been good at dodging and deflecting. Not to mention, cutting and running."

He ignored her taunt. "Did you happen to notice if Thora was still seated with her group when you left?"

"No, but I wasn't keeping tabs."

"Did anyone see you leave?"

"I didn't make an announcement, but I'm a regular at Molly's. If you recall, I'm the one who introduced you to the place. I'm sure if you ask around someone will remember my departure."

Will removed another copy of the computer

rendering from his pocket. "Did you see this man last night? He would have been seated at the bar."

She scanned the image and glanced up. "Who is he?"

"A person of interest," Will said. "We don't yet know his name."

Her anger faded and she once again became a cop. "You think he had something to do with Thora's kidnapping?"

"That's what we're trying to find out."

"I don't remember seeing him, but the rendering is pretty generic." She studied the likeness for another long moment. "Mildly attractive. Hair not too long, not too short. No facial hair, no noticeable scars, piercings or tattoos. He's almost too nondescript. Nothing about him would have stood out in a crowd except for his eyes." She glanced up. "He has that deranged, Charles Manson kind of stare."

Will remembered only too well the concentrated focus of the stranger's gaze as he'd watched Thora in the bar mirror. If only he'd said something, done something. If only he'd stuck around to follow the guy outside.

Elise handed him the rendering and straightened. "I didn't see him. Not that I remember. Are we done now?"

"We're done." He folded the image and stuffed it in his pocket. "Sorry for the interruption." He glanced toward the open window. "I don't blame you for being upset, but—"

"Yes, I know. It's not personal. You're just doing your job." She moved past him to pull back the screen door. "You keep telling yourself that and you might actually start to believe it."

"Elise?"

She paused.

"Why did you tell Claire Hartley you were forced out of Criminal Investigations? I was told you asked to be transferred."

She turned slowly to face him. "Told by whom? You were my commanding officer. You had the last word."

He shrugged. "I thought you'd gone over my head. I didn't make a fuss because it seemed to be what you wanted."

"Then you should have asked *me* what I wanted. But you didn't, did you, Will? It was easier to believe what you wanted to believe."

"It wasn't like that."

Her composure cracked. "It was exactly like that. From the moment you decided to become a cop, the powers-that-be had big plans for you. You were fast-tracked right out of the academy. One advancement after another. The youngest officer to ever make lieutenant and now you're a deputy chief at thirty-five. Unheard of. But not for you. You're their golden boy. A legacy. The handsome son of a fallen hero. You couldn't ask for a more perfect face for the Belfort Police Department. Me? I was just in your way."

Will frowned. "I never thought that."

"Maybe not, but you have to admit my departure smoothed things over for you. No loud-mouthed ex-girlfriend in CID trash-talking your sterling reputation." She pushed open the wooden door and stepped inside, letting the screen door snap shut between them.

"Regardless of what happened between us, I never wanted you to leave Criminal Investigations," Will said. "You were a good detective."

She glared at him through the screen. "I'm still a good detective. Far better than anyone ever gave me credit for."

WILL CIRCLED THE NEIGHBORHOOD, giving Elise enough time to go back inside before he turned down her street and parked behind a utility van at the curb. The neighbor with the water hose took note of his return, but he hoped the large vehicle would give him sufficient cover from the other side of the street in case Elise happened to glance out her front window.

While he waited, he mulled over their conversation. Her bitterness had taken him by surprise, even though Claire had warned him about the chip on Elise's shoulder. Their breakup last year had seemed amicable at the time. She'd pretty much shrugged off his apology and agreed the relationship had run its course. Maybe he'd misread her. Maybe that was another case of him taking the easy way out. Believing what he wanted to believe. Had he really been that much of a clueless jerk? No wonder Elise resented his career advancements. The promotion after their split must have seemed like a slap in the face. But nursing a grudge over a breakup was a far cry from kidnapping his old girlfriend and burying her alive.

If Elise's time line checked out, she'd left the pub before Thora. On the surface, his trip to see her seemed like a monumental waste of time. He'd learned nothing concrete to suggest she was in any way culpable. But something apart from her lingering animosity bothered Will. He'd caught flickers of rage in her eyes. A cold, righteous fury that the whole department had done her wrong on his behalf.

There was also the matter of fresh scratches on her neck and arms…

The shadow of a visitor he'd glimpsed inside her house…

What's going on with you, Elise?

He called the station to check in while he waited. The Tech Unit was still going through the videos. Thora's kidnapper had used an untraceable number to send the text messages, but triangulation had placed the phone downtown at the time they'd been sent, miles away from any wooded areas. Officers were searching dumpsters and gutters near the location in the hopes of finding the discarded burner so that the serial number could be traced back to the point of purchase. That was another long shot. Whoever had taken Thora apparently knew how to cover their tracks. Only one of the security cameras outside the pub had been operational. Whether by luck or careful planning, the kidnapper had managed to evade the working camera.

His gaze shot back to Elise's front door. A man wearing gray slacks and a white shirt stepped out on the porch. He kept his back to the street as he spoke to someone—presumably Elise—through the screen. Will fished in the console for the compact pair of binoculars he kept handy. He lifted them to his eyes and adjusted the focus ring. He still couldn't get a look at the man's face, but his rigid posture suggested the conversation was anything but casual. He stood with his feet slightly apart, hands jammed into his pockets.

After a moment, Elise stepped out on the porch to join him, letting the screen door slam shut behind her. She was fully dressed now in jeans and a white T-shirt. She appeared just as tense as her partner, jabbing her finger in the air as he backed toward the steps. Will rolled down his window but he was too far away to catch anything other than the muted drift of their angry voices on the breeze.

The argument had attracted the neighbor with

the garden hose. She seemed to forget about her task as she stared unabashedly across the street. Then slowly she turned to glance in Will's direction. For an anxious moment, he thought she might head down the sidewalk and give away his position. Instead, she sat down on her porch steps and fanned her face with a straw hat as she pretended to take a breather.

Elise and her companion seemed oblivious to their audience. They argued for several seconds longer and then the man turned and ran down the steps. Elise hurried after him, briefly clutching his arm before he shook her off and strode toward the street. When he emerged from the deep shade of her front yard, Will finally got a look at his face.

He lowered the binoculars and gaped in surprise. *What the hell...?*

Then he lifted them once more and adjusted the focus as he followed the man across the street to a vintage white Mercedes parked beneath an oak tree.

Logan Neville unlocked the car door and climbed inside. He took a moment to put on his sunglasses and check the rearview mirror before he pulled away from the curb. Will slumped in the seat as Neville sped past him but the man stared straight ahead, seemingly intent on making a quick getaway.

Will tracked the car in his mirror until Neville turned at the first intersection and disappeared. Then he straightened, once again toying with the focus ring to bring Elise's front porch into view. She stood at the top of the steps staring back at him.

Chapter Six

With each second that passed, Thora grew weaker. The influx of fresh air from the surface kept her alive, but the heat inside the box had become unbearable. Her legs had started to cramp and hunger pains had long since given way to a fresh wave of nausea. Her skin and clothing were soaked with sweat. Perspiration would help keep her body cooled for now, but she was starting to experience signs of dehydration.

She ran her tongue over her dry lips and tried not to dwell on the passage of each moment. Time simultaneously slowed to a crawl and rushed headlong toward an inevitable conclusion. Without water, the heat would soon do her in. How long since her last drink? Could have been minutes, could have been hours. She had started intermittently drumming on the air tube and lid in the same specific sequence her abductor had used: tap, tap...pause...tap, tap. Nothing had come back to her yet. No answering tap. No trickling water.

No stolen keepsake. Nothing but the rasp of her own breathing to keep her company.

Placing her mouth to the air tube, she drew the warm air slowly into her lungs and tried to stay focused on her self-assigned tasks. Namely, keeping fear and panic at bay while she figured out who had imprisoned her and why. Anything to help keep her sane while she waited for someone to come to her rescue. Or not.

Where are you, Will?

Was he even looking for her yet?

Thora could only guess at the time. Surely enough hours had gone by and her mother would have become concerned when she couldn't reach her. Maddie Graham had always been a worrier and Thora had never been so deeply thankful for her mother's neurosis as she was in that moment. Maddie wouldn't let too much time go by before she notified the police. And if she couldn't get anyone to listen, she'd enlist Claire's help. Her sister had a natural proclivity for drama and contrariness. She wouldn't hesitate to drive back from Houston and raise holy hell if she thought a loved one was in trouble. She wouldn't give up or back down until someone agreed to look for Thora.

As soon as the police found the Volvo at the pub, an alarm would surely be sounded. Or had someone driven her car back to the townhouse to delay discovery of the abduction? What if the kidnapper had used her phone to send reassuring text messages to Claire and her mother? What if nobody would start looking for her until she failed to turn up for brunch with her mother on Sunday? She wouldn't last that long. She might not make it through another day.

Thora still wanted to believe that Will would somehow find her. He had the power, resources and determination to make things happen. But hope had started to dwindle and despair once again needled at her. Where was he at that moment? At the station marshaling his forces, or at home relaxing with a beer and a ball game? Or sleeping in with the woman he'd brought to the pub last night?

Stop obsessing over Will Dresden. Concentrate on the investigation. Figure out who did this to you and why.

Although if she died in the box, did it really matter who had put her there?

Yes, it matters. Puzzle it out.

She ran down a list of questions.

Did you see anyone in the parking lot before you were grabbed? Did you hear anything other than the distorted voice in your ear?

Did anyone follow you out of the pub? Think!

The queasiness pushed up into her throat, making it difficult to breathe through the tube. Through sheer force of will, she forced back the

nausea and rapped on the lid. Tap, tap…pause…
tap, tap.

*Don't waste your energy. The kidnapper isn't
coming back. Now concentrate! Go back to the
beginning. Go back to the pub.*

She closed her eyes and drifted back in time,
back into that crowded, noisy bar with the cloying
smell of perfume and aftershave mingling with
the malty smell of beer. It was like having an
out-of-body experience. Like watching a movie.
Thora could see herself seated at the table with her
colleagues. Everyone was talking and laughing,
having a good time. She observed herself going
through the motions. Sipping her wine. Smiling
politely at the person across the table from her.
Happy on the outside, miserable on the inside.
*Just get up and leave. Go home. Five minutes
can save your life.*

But, of course, she couldn't get up and leave.
She couldn't go back in time and change the
past. The abduction had happened. She was living through it at that very moment. All she could
do was lie on her back in that sweltering box and
try to solve the mystery of her capture.

*Relax. Let the memories unfold without forcing
them. Stay in the pub. Focus on the people with
whom you came into contact. What did you notice about the interactions?*

She had remained seated at the table with her
colleagues for most of the evening, trying to con-

verse over the background noises. She'd only left the table once to visit the ladies' room after finishing her wine. *Never, ever leave a glass unattended in a bar.* She hadn't. At that point in the evening, the drug had yet to be administered, of that she was certain. She'd been steady on her feet and keenly observant as she made her way through the crowd.

Strange how everything had been hazy when she'd first awakened in the box, but now she could remember that walk to the ladies' room so vividly she wondered if she might be dreaming. Or hallucinating.

Focus!

She'd scanned the faces at the bar and taken note of someone coming out of the restroom. She'd even tracked Will and his date out of the corner of her eye. Her situational awareness had remained high at that point. Or so she'd thought. But had she missed something? A figure slipping through the crowd behind her? A lifted phone, a subtle nod to an accomplice?

Except for the unsettling stare of the stranger in the mirror, she'd had no hint of trouble at that point in the evening. Even when someone had entered the restroom behind her, she hadn't been concerned. The pub was busy and there were multiple stalls. People would come in and out all night.

But…who had come in directly behind her?

That struck her as important, so she needed to remember.

She squeezed her eyes closed and tried to corral her scattered thoughts.

Breathe in, breathe out. Relax. Focus.

Yes, now she had it.

When she came out of the stall, a woman with red, curly hair and vivid blue eyes had stood at one of the sinks refreshing her lipstick. She wore large hoop earrings that tangled in her ringlets and a pair of faded jeans that fit her athletic physique like a custom-made glove. As Thora stepped up to the adjoining sink to wash her hands, their gazes met briefly in the mirror.

The hand holding the lipstick tube paused. The redhead said in surprise, "Thora? Thora Graham? Wow. I heard you were back in town, but I never expected to run into you here. How in the world are you?"

"I'm well, thank you." The woman's effusiveness made her uncomfortable. She placed her palms underneath the automatic soap dispenser while she desperately searched her memory banks. The redhead looked familiar, but she couldn't place her and Thora always hated that awkward moment before a name came back to her.

Their gazes met again in the mirror. The woman smiled, but her eyes were coolly assessing. "You don't remember me, do you?"

Thora rinsed her hands and reached for a paper towel. "I'm sorry. I'm terrible with names, but you do look familiar."

"No need to apologize. It's been a long time." The woman finished applying her lipstick and pressed her lips together. "Elise Barrett. You and I were at U-SET together about a hundred years ago. We always seemed to end up in the same criminology classes."

Thora said in relief. "Of course. Elise. It has been a while, hasn't it?" She discarded the paper towel, wondering how long she would be expected to stay and chat. She wanted nothing more than to go back outside, pay for her wine and go home. But wasn't this the kind of thing a normal person was expected to do when returning to her hometown? Reconnect with old acquaintances? For her mother's and sister's sakes—and for her own mental health—she decided to make the effort. She smiled at Elise's reflection. "You've changed your hair. The curls threw me."

Elise wound a corkscrew around one finger and released it. "You wouldn't believe how long it used to take to straighten this mess. I don't bother these days."

"It suits you," Thora said for lack of anything better to contribute.

"Thanks. I guess we've all gone through changes since college, some of them not so trivial." She paused, her attention still captured by

Thora's reflection. "I was sorry to hear about your husband."

Thora frowned. How did Elise Barrett know about Michael? "It was a long time ago."

"Some things you don't get over no matter how much time goes by. It was a car accident, wasn't it?" She must have noticed Thora's closed expression because she looked instantly contrite. "Sorry. Belfort is still a small town in a lot of ways. Your sister and I have mutual friends. You know how it is. People talk."

Maybe she would need to have a word with Claire about discretion. Thora didn't like people prying into her personal life, especially when it came to her dead husband. She considered it a gross violation of his privacy, too, and shutting down idle curiosity was the last and only way she had of protecting him. So she did what she could in the moment, which was to quickly change the subject. "You stayed in Belfort after college?"

Elise sighed. "Yes. I never intended to, but you know what they say about the best laid plans. I was accepted into the police academy after graduation, and I've been with the Belfort PD ever since."

"That's great."

"Is it?" She shrugged. "I started out in Patrol and then worked my way up to detective in the Criminal Investigations Division. Now I'm Internal Affairs. You know, the cop that other cops love to hate."

"I'm sure that's not true."

"Oh, it is. The level of vitriol would surprise you." She dropped the lipstick in her bag and turned to face Thora. "What about you? What made you decide to come back to Belfort after all these years?"

How much longer before she could politely excuse herself and go back to the table? Thora resisted the urge to edge toward the door. "My family still lives here. When the university offered me a position as adjunct professor, I decided it was time for a change."

"From Quantico to Belfort. That's quite a big change," Elise observed. "I would never have expected that of you."

"Why?"

She leaned back against the sink. "You were so passionate about the FBI back in college. You had your future and career all mapped out and you weren't about to let anything or anyone stop you."

Even the love of my life. "As you said, the best laid plans."

Elise cocked her head. "You don't find it boring? Surely teaching at a small college in the armpit of Texas can't compete with the work you did at the FBI."

Thora had a feeling the woman was fishing

for some kind of response. The conversation was starting to drift from uncomfortable into disquieting, but possibly she was overreacting. She'd forgotten how casually nosy people in small towns could be. Well-meaning for the most part, but invasive nonetheless.

"You seem to have the wrong idea about my work," she said. "Most of my time was spent researching and analyzing data in a basement cubicle. It was rewarding but rarely exciting."

Elise looked skeptical. "I find that hard to believe. From what I hear, you were involved in at least one intense manhunt that spanned the better part of a decade. I can't imagine what it would be like to devote that many years of your life to tracking a monster like the Weatherman. It must have seemed at times like you were trapped in a nightmare."

"You learn to cope."

"I guess." Elise gave an exaggerated shudder. "I read somewhere that you were instrumental in his capture. You were the one who alerted the local authorities to be on the lookout for an underground bunker or storm cellar on his property. Turns out, that's exactly where he was hiding."

"You seem to know quite a lot about the case," Thora noted.

Elise smiled. "I'll admit to a particular fascination for the Weatherman. Our proximity to I-10 makes it likely that he traveled through Belfort dozens if not hundreds of times during his killing sprees. There was even speculation that he might have a dumping ground around here somewhere. I've often wondered if I might have encountered him at some point, in a bar or convenience store. You never know."

"It's possible," Thora said.

"From what I've read, he's extremely charismatic and manipulative. Have you ever met him?"

"No."

She looked surprised. "I would have thought you'd want to talk to him if for no other reason than to satisfy your curiosity."

"I know all I need to know about James Ellis Ridgeway," Thora replied.

Elise gave a vague nod. "Can I ask you a question?"

Thora had tried very hard to put that case behind her, but the Weatherman was all anyone ever wanted to talk about when they found out who she was and what she did. She nodded politely.

"During the time you were hunting Ridgeway, did you ever worry that he might also be tracking you?"

"What do you mean?"

"He's intelligent and surprisingly sophisticated for his level of education. He claimed to have contacts in various law enforcement agencies all across the country, including the FBI. That's how he eluded capture for so many years. If he knew about you, about your work, what would have stopped him from coming after you? Hypothetically speaking, of course."

"A lot of people worked that case," Thora said. "Why would he target me?"

"Because you were the one who had him all figured out."

Her definitive tone sent an inexplicable chill up Thora's spine. "That's giving me too much credit. Or too little, depending on your perspective. If I had him all figured out, I would hope we'd have caught him a lot sooner than we did."

"I see your point, but still." Her smile seemed cagey, as if her outer friendliness didn't quite match her internal motivation. "I think I would have had a hard time sleeping at night knowing he was out there. Especially after your husband died. Did you ever wonder if Ridgeway might have somehow been responsible for the accident?"

The notion jarred Thora even though the thought had crossed her mind from time to time. The local police and her colleagues at the Bureau had assured her Michael's car accident was just that—an accident. The driver that hit him had fled the scene and was found days later in his garage with a self-inflicted gunshot wound to his head. The investigation had revealed a long history of alcohol and substance abuse, multiple DUIs, driving with a suspended license—case closed. But something hadn't seemed quite right to Thora. At the time, Ridgeway was still three years away from capture. It wasn't as unlikely as some of her colleagues wanted her to believe that he'd uncovered her identity.

"Food for thought." Elise straightened from the sink. "Not to change the subject, but have you talked to Will Dresden since you've been home? You two were pretty tight back in the day."

"That was back in the day," Thora said. "We didn't keep in touch after college."

"Then you don't know—"

The door swung open and one of the young women who'd been involved in the earlier altercation came in. Baylee Fisher froze, her hand still on the door as her gaze darted back and forth from Thora to Elise.

She focused in on Elise for a moment before she said, "Sorry. Am I interrupting something?"

"Not at all." Thora turned back to Elise. "It was nice catching up."

The redhead nodded. "I'm sure we'll see each other again soon."

THE MEMORIES WERE coming fast and furious now, but Thora wasn't sure she could trust her recall. She was in bad shape mentally and physically. Her mouth, lips and eyes had gone dry. Her head pounded and she had intermittent spells of dizziness and confusion. All signs of dehydration and heat stroke. For all she knew, her memories might well be hallucinations. Sometimes they were almost too raw and intense. But whether real or fantasy, the visions were the only thing keeping her calm when the instinct for survival demanded that she claw her way out of the box. She knew that even the slightest physical exertion would use up too much air and energy and yet she still had to guard against a natural inclination to fight.

She lay motionless with her hands balled at her sides and gave herself a pep talk. She could do this. Above all else, she had to remain focused. She had to be smart. She was running out of time and she still hadn't figured out the identity of her kidnapper. She'd come into contact with a number of people at the pub and as far as she was concerned, all were suspects. But the name that had popped into her head when she'd first awakened in the box was Logan Neville. That had to mean something. *Dig deeper.*

Returning to the table after her trip to the restroom, she'd had every intention of saying goodnight to her colleagues. To her chagrin, Neville had seated himself next to her. If her drink had, in fact, been drugged, his proximity in hindsight seemed significant, if not downright ominous.

Thora struggled to recall the details of their brief encounter. She must have ordered a second glass of wine at some point, but why would she have done so when she'd been determined to leave? Something about a toast...

Yes, that was it. Before she could escape, Neville had insisted on making a birthday toast to the colleague for whom the celebration was in honor. He'd called for a fresh round of drinks for everyone at the table, which was how Thora had ended up with a second glass of wine. The logical place to spike a drink without notice was at the bar, but Neville's positioning himself in the chair next to her now seemed deliberately strategic. Thora had sipped gingerly. Was that why she hadn't experienced immediate side effects? Because the drug had entered her system in such minute amounts?

Had she noticed anything dubious in Neville's conduct? Had he distracted her at any point? Or had he seated himself at her side so that he could monitor her reaction to the already drugged wine? Thora tried to analyze his behavior in retrospect. Had he watched her closely as she drank, perhaps losing patience when she allowed the liquid to barely touch her lips?

"I feel we've gotten off on the wrong foot," he'd said after the toast. "I've always believed in the direct approach so I'm just going to come right out and ask. Have I said or done something to offend you?"

"Why would you think that?"

"Call it intuition." The corners of his mouth twitched. "You don't like me much, do you?"

She shrugged. "I hardly know you. I don't have feelings for you one way or another."

"That's blunt, but I appreciate your honesty. Maybe you would be better able to form an opinion if you didn't spend so much of your time alone in your office."

Was he hitting on her? The very thought made Thora cringe. He was elegant and attractive in a scholarly sort of way, but his appeal was lost on her. "When I'm on campus, I like to work," she said. "It's nothing personal."

He picked up his glass of scotch. "Let me try this again. I'm hoping we can bury the hatchet over a drink. I'll be the first to admit, I haven't been as welcoming as I should have been. My only excuse is that I'm an old dog and we tend to be a bit territorial."

His candor surprised her. "I'm not here to upset the status quo. My contract is only for a year. We don't have to be friends, but we don't need to be enemies, either."

"To keeping the peace." He clicked his glass against hers, then raised the scotch to his lips, pausing for a fraction of a second until she did the same. He returned his drink to the table and wrapped both hands around the glass as he studied her with a curious smile. "Now that we've sufficiently wiped the slate clean, I wonder if I could ask a favor."

Thora was immediately on guard. "That all depends on what the favor is."

"I have a podcast called *Exploring the Criminal Mind.* Our guests span the gamut from writers to forensic experts to psychics. I'm sure you've heard of it. It's become quite popular in recent months."

He didn't frame it as a question, but an assumption that, yes, of course she knew of his podcast and all his other impressive endeavors. "I've heard of it."

"Would you be willing to come on as a guest?"

She hadn't expected that. He'd taken her completely by surprise. "That's…really not my kind of thing."

"Oh, I think with your experience and expertise it could be exactly your sort of thing. Think of it as a lively, sometimes controversial chat among peers. You'd be surprised how quickly an hour can fly by."

"I'm sure it would be interesting, but like I said, not my thing."

He seemed reluctant to take no for an answer. "You might change your mind when you hear the topic. I'll be interviewing a freelance journalist who's writing a book about the Weatherman."

"Is that so?" Now Thora understood his persistence.

"He's followed the case for years and has formulated some interesting theories regarding Ridgeway and his victims. Aside from you, he probably knows more about the Weatherman and his modus operandi than anyone else in the world. The two of you together would make for a dynamic discussion."

"I'm afraid my answer is still no."

"What if I told you this reporter recently visited Ridgeway at the Donaldson Correctional Facility in Alabama?" His tone sounded conspiratorial. "Would you be at all interested in *that* conversation?"

"Not really. I've heard all I need to from James Ellis Ridgeway."

Neville leaned in. "What if I told you that your name was mentioned in the course of their visit?"

Her heart thudded. "In what way?"

"Be a guest on my podcast and find out."

She couldn't tell if he was bluffing or not, but something told her she was being baited. "I don't speak publicly about any of the cases I've worked on, in particular the Weatherman. I have a rule against glamorizing monsters."

He looked as if he wanted to argue, but then he shrugged. "That's a pity. There's so much to be gleaned from predators like Ridgeway and from the hunters who track them." He lifted his drink, observing her over the rim of his glass. "Hunters like you."

Something flickered in his eyes before he could disguise the emotion behind his smile. The brief lapse unnerved Thora and she reminded herself that Logan Neville wasn't to be trusted.

"I never thought of myself as anything more than an analyst," she said.

Whatever she'd glimpsed behind his smile was gone. He said without a hint of guile, "Which is exactly why I'd like to ask another favor. My team and I are currently working on a cold case that the local police, in their typical fashion, badly bungled. A nine-year-old boy disappeared on his way home from school. The child vanished in broad daylight on a crowded street. The investigators concentrated so much of their time and effort on the boy's stepfather that they let the trail go cold. I've obtained copies of the official police file. Whether you agree to do my podcast or not, I wonder if you'd be willing to take a look at the case."

"How did you get a copy of the file?"

"Mostly by submitting a request, but the file I have is incomplete. It seems there are sealed records connected to the case. If I told you I have a confidential source in the department willing to provide access, would you take a look?"

"I'll think about it," Thora said.

"Don't take too long. I'll be going away for a few days and I'd like to have an answer before I leave. The boy's family has been in limbo for ten years. They deserve justice. And the lead detective that botched the case finally needs to be held to account. Instead, he's been elevated to the position of deputy chief."

Thora said in shock, "Are you talking about Will Dresden?"

A brow lifted. "Why, yes. Do you know him?"

"I used to."

"Then your insight could be invaluable. You know where to find me when you make a decision."

The conversation had ended abruptly. Neville had excused himself from the table and rejoined Addison March at the bar. They made very little effort to disguise the intimate nature of their relationship. Neville's hand had rested at the small of the young woman's back as she'd leaned in to whisper in his ear. While she spoke to him, her gaze had vectored in on Thora and she'd stared boldly before turning to disappear into the back room. Neville took out his phone, thumbed a text message and then followed her.

Upon reflection, it all seemed choreographed to Thora. And very suspect. The brief conversation with Logan Neville. The chance meeting in the bathroom with Elise Barrett. Even the scuffle between Addison March and Baylee Fisher earlier in the evening. Everything had meaning. Thora could look back now and recognize the undercurrents flowing in the pub throughout the evening. At the time, though, she'd been oblivious to anything but her desire to escape the noise and go home.

She'd left her wine unfinished, settled her tab and stood. The slight dizziness had been her first clue that all was not well. Why hadn't it occurred to her then that she'd been drugged? *Because no one believes it will happen to them.* Even someone with her training and experience could fall victim to a false sense of security. All she remembered feeling in that moment was relief that the evening had finally come to an end. And if she were truthful, she'd thought about Will and his companion. She'd wondered in passing if they'd gone to his place or hers and how serious they might be.

None of her business, of course. She'd had her chance with Will Dresden. *You can't go home again.*

Except she had and look where it had gotten her. She pressed her hand against the top of the container, confirming to herself that her captivity wasn't a hallucination or a dream. The box was real. Would her captor come back with more water or had she been abandoned for good? Tap, tap… pause…tap, tap. *Keep at it.* Tap, tap…pause…tap, tap. Each sequence more desperate than the last.

Even the air from the pipe couldn't keep her alive for long. Little by little she felt herself slipping away. The only way to save herself was to mentally leave the box.

She pictured herself once more in the pub, making her way through the crowd to the entrance. Had someone followed her out? Wait…*wait*…

Someone had tailed her to the door and called her name. She'd turned so quickly the room had started to spin. A female face swam before her. Slowly the young woman's features came into focus.

"Professor Graham? Are you okay? You don't look so good." When Thora didn't answer, the woman said, "It's Baylee Fisher. I was in your Psychology of Criminal Behavior class. Tuesdays and Thursdays? I was wondering if I could have a word."

"I was just on my way out—"

"I don't mean *here*!" She quickly glanced around. "Maybe we could meet in your office."

"You can stop by on Monday morning."

"I don't think this can wait." She sounded anxious, almost frightened. "I overheard something I shouldn't have. I wouldn't bother you except…" She cast another furtive glance over her shoulder. "This might be *really* important."

"Be at my office at nine tomorrow morning. I don't usually take meetings on Saturday, but I'll make an exception."

Baylee looked relieved. "Thank you." She backed away. "Just one more thing. *Be careful.*"

With that, she was gone.

The memory flitted away.

Thora lay in the box and berated herself for not having remembered the cryptic warning earlier, but she had little control over the amnesia. Her memories came and went. She was still laboring under the influence of the drug. She felt feverish, delirious. *Will, where are you?*

He isn't coming. Why should he? You left him, remember? You chose your career over him. What makes you think he's even looking for you?

Yes, I chose my career, and I've regretted that decision for thirteen long years.

She couldn't allow herself to think that way. It seemed disloyal to Michael's memory. He'd been a good husband and she'd loved him. She wouldn't betray what they'd had by thinking about another man in her last hours.

Instead, she concentrated on compiling a list of suspects, Logan Neville and the stranger at the bar being the two most obvious. She added anyone else she could remember from the pub, including Elise Barrett, Addison March and Baylee Fisher. And reluctantly, she added James Ellis Ridgeway.

With the last of her waning strength, she tried to determine means, motive and opportunity for each of the suspects, but a disturbing thought suddenly occurred to her. What if the kidnapper had never set foot in the pub? What if her abduction had been completely random? A case of being in the wrong place at the wrong time like so many of James Ellis Ridgeway's victims. That would complicate her investigation immeasurably. That would make figuring out who had abducted her in the time she had left next to impossible.

Chapter Seven

Will was on his way back to the station when he got a call from Thora's neighbor. After she explained who she was, she said in a low, anxious tone, "You said to call if that guy showed up again. The one I saw outside the townhouse next door. He's here right now."

Will's hands tightened around the wheel as he automatically checked the rearview mirror. "What's he doing?"

"I can't see him at the moment. But when he first walked up, he rang Thora's doorbell. Then he went around the building. He hasn't come back yet."

"But you think he's still on the premises?"

"Unless he took the long way around to get back to the parking lot." She hesitated, then said. "I have a question for you, Deputy Chief. Some police officers were here earlier. I recognized the CSU patches on their uniforms. They came with all their cases and they stayed for quite some time. I'm sorry, but before we go any further, I'd really like to know what is going on. I'm right next door, and I live alone. Should I be worried?"

"There's no reason to think you're in any danger," Will said.

"That's not very reassuring. Can you at least tell me what happened to Thora? That's her name, right? Is she—"

"She's alive. That's all I can say at the moment."

The neighbor expelled a sharp breath. "I think you just told me more than you meant to. Did this guy do something to her?"

"Right now, we just want to talk to him."

"If he's harmed her and the police know it, why would he come back to her house?"

"I need you to stay focused," Will said. "Take a breath and stay on the phone. I'm going to put you on hold while I get a patrol car over to your complex." He used the radio in his vehicle to alert dispatch while he whipped off the road into a parking lot and turned in the direction of the townhouses. "Okay," he said to the neighbor. "Tell me exactly what you saw when he came to the door. It's important."

"I was at my front window when the police left. I'm not usually the nosy sort. I don't care what my neighbors do as long as they leave me alone. But a Crime Scene Unit gets your attention, particularly after our earlier visit. They loaded up their cases, got in a van and drove away. That's when I spotted him coming up the walkway. I don't think the timing was a coincidence. He must have been watching her townhouse and waiting for the police to leave."

"Did you see his vehicle this time?"

"No. I'm guessing he either parked outside the gate or in front of another building. Which, in itself, seems sketchy."

"Are you sure he was the same man you saw last Thursday?"

"I'm one hundred percent positive. I don't forget faces and I got a good look at him both times. He was dressed the same as before—nice pants and shirt, hair longish and kind of messy. If you only saw him in passing, you wouldn't think twice about him. But I noticed two things straightaway. He acted like he was in a hurry, and he kept glancing over his shoulder as if he thought someone might be following him. Or maybe he was worried about being seen in front of Thora's townhouse. My first inclination was to go outside and confront him. A gated community is supposed to keep out creeps like him. But then I remembered my previous impression and thought better of it. As I said, I live alone and guys like that are unpredictable."

"You did the right thing," Will said. "Has he come back around to the front of the complex yet?"

"Hold on, let me take a look." She was only gone for a couple of seconds. "I can't see him, but something just occurred to me. He probably rang Thora's doorbell just to make sure all the cops were gone. He already knew she wasn't home. If someone had come to the door, he would have given them the same line he tried to feed me the other day. He's an old friend, been trying to get in touch, etcetera. I bet the reason he went around the building was to try and find a way inside. Each unit has a walled courtyard in the back. He could break a window and no one would see him." She lowered her voice as if afraid of being overheard in her own place. "For all we know, he could already be inside her house."

She was starting to get a little worked up again so Will said, "Don't worry. I'm only a few minutes away and the first patrol car should be pulling up at the complex any second now. In the meantime, stay inside and lock your doors. And keep away from the windows. Whatever you do, don't confront him. He isn't after you, but you're right to worry that he could be unpredictable. We also don't want to tip him off before we have officers on the scene."

"Okay, just please make sure he doesn't come back here again. I don't like the idea of that guy skulking about the grounds. I have a hard enough time sleeping at night."

Will ended the call and tossed his phone aside as he checked his mirrors and changed lanes. His foot was heavy on the accelerator, but Saturday afternoon traffic had started to back up on the main thoroughfare. He took as many shortcuts and backstreets as he could and arrived before the first patrol car. Not surprising since almost every available unit had been reassigned to search for Thora.

Entering the gate code on the keypad, he let himself in and parked next to the neighbor's car directly in front of Thora's building. He pocketed his phone, checked his firearm and approached the building cautiously, using the lush landscaping as cover. Easing up to the front window, he glanced inside, then jerked back when he caught sight of a moving shadow.

He waited a few seconds, then chanced another glance. The man stood with his back to the window going through Thora's desk. Will retreated and tried the front door. It was locked. Which meant whoever was inside Thora's townhouse had probably broken a rear window as the neighbor suspected.

Will hurried around the building, pausing to check his surroundings as he approached the gate. No one was around. Under the circumstances, that was a good thing. Bystanders were always a worry.

Peering through the iron rods into the courtyard, he scanned the enclosed area. He didn't see any broken glass on the brick floor, but the back door stood ajar. Unless the CSU team had left it open, which was unlikely, the suspect had either jimmied the door or picked the lock.

He released the latch and the gate swung inward on creaking hinges. The sound stopped him cold, and he waited a beat before entering the courtyard. Sensing an unwelcome presence, a dog in a nearby unit started to bark. Between the excited canine and the squeaky gate, Will had little hope of a stealthy approach. He flattened himself against the outside wall and listened as he unholstered his weapon. The smart play here was to stay put and wait for backup. He had no idea what he might walk into. But if the intruder had heard the dog and the gate, he might get spooked, go out the front door and get to his vehicle before Will could catch him. He wouldn't take that risk. Not when every second was so vitally important to Thora's survival.

Pushing the door open with his toe, Will entered silently and eased through the small laundry room into the kitchen. The townhouse was an open concept design. From the kitchen, he could see straight through the dining room into the living room, but he'd yet to catch another glimpse of the intruder. If he rushed the room, he might still have the element of surprise, but he had no way of knowing whether or not the man was armed. Or whether or not he'd heard Will's approach. He had to assume the affirmative on both counts.

Bracing his weapon with his left hand, he

moved quickly through the dining room and into the living room, drawing a bead on the spot where he'd last seen the intruder. No one was at the desk. Will spun, taking in every nook and cranny of the room before moving into the foyer. He checked the front door. Locked. His gaze lifted to the top of the staircase. The suspect must have gone up to the second floor. Did he know Will was in the house or had he gone upstairs looking for something?

Will glanced out the front window. Still no sign of backup, but patrol cars would surely arrive on the scene any minute now. He could plant himself in the living room and wait for the intruder to come back downstairs or he could go up after him. He went up, his footsteps silenced by a thick runner on the hardwood steps. He checked the guest bathroom at the top of the stairs, the first bedroom and then moved down the hallway to Thora's room. He could hear sounds from inside as the man rummaged through her things.

Weapon still drawn, Will planted himself in the doorway. "Police! Don't move. Stay right where you are."

The man was halfway out the open window. He paused and glanced back. Will recognized him instantly as the stranger from the pub. The dark eyes and probing stare were unmistakable.

Will checked the corners of the room from his periphery as he entered. Satisfied that he was dealing with only one suspect, he said, "Move away from the window and keep your hands where I can see them."

The man's gaze remained riveted on Will. He didn't look so much concerned as extremely focused, waiting for an opportunity. "If you want to talk, we can talk, but please put away the weapon first. I don't like guns and we both know you're not going to shoot me, anyway."

His response only served to tick Will off. Anger and adrenaline in a tense situation were never a good mix so he made sure his emotions were firmly under control as he advanced. "You sound awfully certain for a guy staring down the barrel of one of those guns you don't like."

The man's gaze never wavered. "You won't shoot because I have something you want."

"And what is that?"

"Put away the weapon, and I'll tell you."

His smugness wasn't altogether unwarranted. Even if he were to attack, Will would do everything in his power to subdue him without firing a shot. He wasn't about to take out the one person who might be able to lead him to Thora. But the guy's confidence needed to be shaken. "Tell me where she is first and then I'll put away the gun." When the suspect remained unresponsive, Will took aim. "You tell me where she is right now!"

Dead silence.

Will said in a calmer voice, "I don't have to kill

you. I can shoot you in a place that will just make you wish you were dead."

"I don't think you'll risk it."

"Try me."

The stranger hesitated for a split second, then pushed away from the window and jumped. Will lunged across the room and glanced down. It was a long way to the ground. He was hoping the fall would temporarily disable or at least slow the man's escape, but he was already scrambling to his feet, apparently unharmed. Another few seconds and he'd be gone. Will did the only thing he could do. He holstered his weapon, swung his body through the window and leaped two stories to the ground behind the suspect. The banana trees broke his fall, but the impact still hurt. Time enough later to worry about injuries. Springing to his feet, he checked his surroundings. The suspect had headed across the landscaped grounds toward the common area and the parking lot beyond. Will took off in a dead run after him.

Hurdling over a metal bench and sprinting around the bank of mailboxes, he tackled the man at the edge of the parking lot. They hit the pavement hard with a barrage of expletives. The second bone-jarring jolt seemed to take the fight out of the suspect. Will rolled him to this stomach and cuffed him. Then he jerked him to his feet, patted him down and spun him around. There was still no doubt in his mind that he was the stranger from the pub.

The adrenaline still spiraled through Will's veins. He took a moment to grapple with his baser instincts as he fished a wallet from the suspect's pocket and checked his ID. If this guy had taken Thora and buried her alive, Will needed to keep his cool in order to get as much information from him as quickly as possible.

"You're Noah Asher?"

"I am."

He held up a current Alabama driver's license. "You still live at this address?"

"I do."

Will closed the wallet but didn't return it. "You're a long way from home, Mr. Asher."

"Farther than you think," he said.

"Meaning?"

He smiled. "Distance isn't always measured in miles, Detective."

"It's Deputy Chief and that's cryptic."

"For some, maybe."

They stood face-to-face for a moment, staring one another down in silence. Then suddenly, it was as if a switch had been flipped. The stranger's demeanor subtly altered, like a chameleon changing colors right before Will's eyes. His expression softened and his posture relaxed. In the space of a heartbeat, the arrogant miscreant in the window seemed to have transformed into a slightly awkward, more compliant everyman. The unlikely metamorphosis fascinated Will. It was almost as if he stood facing an entirely different person. Almost. But even the most sophisticated con man had a tell, and Will knew enough to look for the signs. The glimmer of cold calculation at the back of the eyes. The uncontrollable twitch at the corners of the mouth.

He also knew better than to let down his guard. If anything, he grew more cautious. The guy was up to something. Will could almost see the wheels turning inside his head as he tried to figure a way out of an arrest.

Will gave him a prompt. "This will all go a lot easier if you just tell me where she is."

Asher dropped his gaze. "I don't know what you're talking about."

"Really? Because you seemed to know before you jumped out that window."

"You surprised me. I said the first thing that popped in my head."

"Just to refresh your memory, you said I wouldn't risk shooting you because you have something I want." Will's voice hardened. "Did you take her?"

"Take who?"

"Enough with the games," Will said in frustration. "You're wasting my time. You know damn well who I'm talking about. Why were you in her townhouse just now?"

Asher looked as if he wanted to keep dodging Will's questions, then decided a little cooperation might be better for his immediate well-being. "It's not what you think."

"Then start talking. You were caught red-handed breaking into a private residence. From my view, things don't look too good for you at the moment."

"I didn't break in. The back door was already open when I got here. The police had just searched the premises, so I didn't see the harm in having a look around. It wasn't like I was going to contaminate evidence or anything."

"If you knew the police were here, then you must have been watching her place."

"No, I—"

"I wouldn't lie to me again if I were you."

He closed his eyes briefly and nodded. "Okay, yes. I waited for the police to leave and then I found a way in. But I wasn't going to take anything."

"Then why go in?"

"I'm a freelance journalist. I was looking for a story. I *swear* I didn't break in."

"Does the term unlawful entry mean anything to you?"

"I may have trespassed, but that's hardly the crime of the century." He turned slightly to the side to display his cuffed hands. "I hurt my arm when you tackled me. Are these really necessary? You have my word I won't try to run."

"You ran before so the cuffs stay on," Will said. "Let's try this again. What did you mean when you said you have something I want?"

Those wheels started to grind again. He took a moment to consider his answer. "I have information that might prove useful to your investigation."

"What kind of information?"

He was still fidgeting with the cuffs. "Are you sure you won't reconsider?"

"You're lucky I don't put you in leg irons," Will said. "You're fine. Just relax your arms. What kind of information?"

A lock of hair fell across his forehead and he tossed back his head. "I wasn't entirely truthful before."

Shocker, Will thought. "Go on."

"I know about Thora Graham's abduction, but I didn't take her. I would never hurt anyone. I have a police scanner app on my phone. There's been a lot of chatter about her abduction all morning. It's not illegal to monitor police broadcasts in the state of Texas," he hastened to point out. "It's also not hard to follow along if you know the standard codes, which I do. I've been covering the crime beat for years as a reporter. I don't know where Ms. Graham is, but I may know who took her."

Will didn't know whether to believe him or not. He could sense he was being played, but to what end, he had no idea. "Tell me everything you know starting with a name."

Asher ignored the instructions and began with a shrug. "It's more of a hunch than anything else, but I have reason to believe her disappearance has something to do with a case she worked on at the FBI."

"Which case?"

"Are you familiar with the serial killer they call the Weatherman?"

Cold dread prickled at Will's nape. "I'm familiar enough. Last I heard, he was sitting on death row in Alabama. Which happens to be where you're from. I'm guessing that's not a coincidence. What's he—and you—got to do with Thora Graham's abduction?"

"She was the FBI analyst who helped the local PD in Mobile take him down."

Will scrutinized Asher's features. He didn't trust the man. Nor did he accept at face value anything coming out of his mouth. The guy found himself in a tough spot. He'd likely say or do anything to take the heat off. But there was a reason he'd been in Thora's house and Will needed to keep chipping away until he uncovered the truth. "You're saying Ridgeway is behind Thora's abduction?"

"I'm saying he could be. I'd put the probability as extremely high. I've followed his case for years, even before his capture. I've written about him extensively. Two weeks ago, I drove to the Donaldson Correctional Facility in Jefferson County to interview him. He talked a lot about the manhunt that eventually led to his arrest and conviction and how he was able to elude the authorities for years by making friends with people in all walks of life, including law enforcement personnel. He was surprisingly candid. And quite credible for a serial killer. I can see why he's so dangerous. He's intelligent and compelling."

"He's also a pathological liar," Will pointed out.

"That, too. Thora Graham's name came up in the course of the conversation. He knows about her role in his capture, and he's aware of her departure from the Bureau. I suspect he knows a lot more than he let on. He seems to have something of a fascination for Ms. Graham. He insinuated the two of them have unfinished business."

The thought of Ridgeway in his cell obsessing over Thora made Will's skin crawl. "He said that to you?"

"Essentially, yes."

"And I suppose you want me to believe you came all this way to warn her. It's just another coincidence she disappeared when you hit town."

"I don't expect you to believe anything, but I'm telling you Thora Graham is only part of the reason I'm here. I came because I was invited to be a guest on a popular podcast to promote my upcoming book."

Will lifted a brow. "So you're a novelist now?"

"True crime. *Storm Warning* chronicles nearly a decade of my personal coverage of the Weatherman."

"Clever title," Will said dryly.

"I know it's cliché, but you have to give the public what they want."

"You think the public is eager for a book about James Ellis Ridgeway?"

"I know they are. The fascination for serial killers hasn't waned. You just have to reach the right audience."

"And you came all this way to do a podcast?"

"It's a popular broadcast and the host thought it would be more effective if we conducted the interview face-to-face rather than remotely. Now I'm starting to wonder if *he* had an ulterior motive for luring me down here."

An answer for everything. "Who's the host?"

"A man named Neville."

That stopped Will for a moment. "Logan Neville?"

"Yes, why? Do you know him?"

"We've crossed paths," Will said.

"Then you must also know he's a professor at the same local university that recently hired Thora Graham. I'm starting to believe there are a lot of interconnected and overlapping threads to this story. And a lot of players moving around in the shadows. Nothing is as it seems, Deputy Chief."

"Including you," Will said. "If you came to Thora's townhouse looking for a story *after* you heard about her abduction, explain to me why you were spotted outside her townhouse two days before she was taken and again last night at the pub where she was last seen. You seem to have more than a passing interest in Thora Graham yourself."

"I wasn't stalking her if that's what you're implying. I freely admit I've been trying to reach her. That's not the same thing."

"Why were you trying to reach her?"

"Partly to tell her about Ridgeway, but also to ask for an interview for my book. She's elusive. To my knowledge, she's never spoken publicly about the Weatherman case."

"Maybe she just wants to be left alone," Will said. "Did that thought ever cross your mind?"

"She's got a story to tell, and I'd like to help her tell it. Taking down James Ellis Ridgeway wasn't without cost. She lost her husband during the course of the manhunt. She also suffered what used to be referred to as a nervous breakdown."

Will's gaze narrowed. "What are you talking about?"

"I don't know the details. I just heard the rumors. The reason she left the Bureau is because she had some kind of episode. That's all I know."

The direction of the conversation made Will uncomfortable. He hated the invasion of Thora's privacy. For all he knew, Asher had made the whole thing up, but something was starting to niggle. "You're telling me you have sources that close to Thora Graham?"

"I keep my ear to the ground like any good reporter learns to do," Asher said. "I ask questions and people tell me things."

"You hear things all the way from Quantico, Virginia?"

"From all over. This is the information age. Word travels fast when you know where to look and how to listen."

He's right about that. In just the thirteen years Will had been in law enforcement, technology had revolutionized data collection and surveillance. The sheer volume of information that could be acquired and exchanged in a narrow time frame was sometimes mind-boggling. He didn't put a lot of credence in the rest of Noah Asher's claim, but he couldn't afford to dismiss it out of hand, either. Something Maddie Graham had told him that morning came back to him. She'd indicated a concern that Thora had returned to Belfort for reasons other than to be close to her family.

The information only mattered to the case because Thora's current mental state was critical to her survival. Will had to believe she was strong enough to get through this. She'd always been tough and determined and she'd been trained by the best in the world. Beyond those known facts, he wouldn't allow himself to speculate.

He returned his attention to Asher. "So regardless of her wishes, you set your sights on an interview. And you weren't going to take no for an answer."

Asher frowned, sensing a trap. "I wouldn't put it that way."

"When you couldn't reach her at her home or on the phone, you decided to follow her to the pub. You were seen watching her from the bar. And now you've unlawfully entered her premises." Will paused. "That sounds a lot like stalking to me."

"You're mischaracterizing everything I just said," Asher protested. "You're presenting my actions in the worst possible light."

"Then tell me the truth. Why were you in her house just now? It wasn't curiosity. You were looking for something besides a story."

He tossed back that pesky lock of hair while he seemed to consider his answer. "I thought I might find evidence."

"Of her disappearance?"

"Of the Weatherman's involvement." He glanced around nervously as if worried the incarcerated killer might have someone close by listening in. "I've talked to Ridgeway. I've seen firsthand how he's able to control and manipulate the prison guards. He could have enlisted any one of them to abduct Thora Graham. Or if not a guard, then someone else on the outside. Someone from his former life, perhaps. I thought whoever took her might have left a calling card, something so subtle the police would have overlooked it."

"Ridgeway never left a calling card," Will said.

"That we know of. If he's behind the abduction, he'd want to find a way to take credit." He turned to stare at Thora's townhouse and Will could have sworn he saw a shudder go through him.

"You're quick on your feet. I'll give you that," Will said. "No shortage of ready answers."

Asher tried to look sincere. "I realize how far-fetched all this must sound, and you've no reason to take my word for any of it. But you can check my credentials for yourself. I'll give you the names and phone numbers of my agent, my publisher, my neighbors—anyone you want to talk to. Even my sister if that would make you feel better. Just please try to keep an open mind. For all we know, Ridgeway could have planned this whole thing to make me look suspicious."

"Well, you do look suspicious," Will agreed. "How do I know you're not the one working with Ridgeway? You've spent time with him. You're writing a book about him. Maybe you're the one who's fallen under his spell."

"A reasonable conclusion, but would I have told you as much as I have if I were working with him?"

"Yes. I think that's exactly what you would do. Which is why I'm taking you in," Will said. "You can cool your heels at the station while I check out your story. You better hope I don't find inconsistencies."

"You won't. I'm telling you the truth."

"Then you've got nothing to worry about." He held up Asher's wallet. "I'll hold onto this in the meantime."

A black-and-white pulled through the gate and wheeled into the parking lot. Will watched as two uniforms got out and headed their way. He turned back to Asher. "Before I turn you over to these fine officers, there's still one thing you haven't explained. If you're innocent, why did you run?"

He answered without hesitation, "It seemed the prudent thing to do. You were holding a gun on me. I had no idea who you were."

"I identified myself as police."

"Yes, but for all I knew, you or someone in your department could have been working with Ridgeway. Take a moment to consider my situation. What if I'm right about him? If you take me in, I'll be a sitting duck."

"You'll be protected. We won't let anything happen to you."

"The way law enforcement protected his other victims? You'll understand if I'm not reassured. Why not let me go and put a tail on me? If I'm innocent, no harm done. If I'm guilty, I could lead you to Thora Graham."

"Tempting, but I'm not done with you yet.

You'll be easier to keep track of at the station. We'll put you in a cell where no one can get to you. You broke the law. You're not walking away from this."

"Then my blood will be on your hands."

Will nodded to the officers coming up behind Asher. "Take him straight downtown. No stops along the way, and don't let him talk to anyone. No one goes in or out of his cell until I get there."

One of the officers took his arm. Asher tried to shake him off. "You're making a big mistake."

The officer tightened his grip. "That's what they all say, buddy."

Asher kept glancing over his shoulder as if he expected Will to change his mind and intervene. He didn't. Instead, he turned and surveyed Thora's building from the parking lot. The images running through his head left him in a cold sweat. He had a terrible feeling that no matter what he did, he'd always be one step behind the kidnapper.

And time was running out. A voice in his head still whispered the same warning: *Hurry, Will. She's dying.*

Chapter Eight

Wake up, Thora. WAKE UP!

The voice was so loud and distinct, she thought for a moment someone had opened the lid of the box and crawled inside with her.

"Will? Is that you?"

No answer.

She tapped the sequence on the air tube. "Will, are you up there? Please, can you hear me?"

Silence.

"Will!"

He didn't answer because he wasn't there. No one was there. The voice hadn't been real. But for one split second, Thora had been certain he'd found her.

Hope drained quickly and she wanted to sob in despair. Instead, she hardened herself to the anguish, refusing to give in to the debilitating gloom even for a moment. She might only be clinging to sanity by a thread. If she started to cry, she might never stop. If she started to scream, she wouldn't be able to stop. She felt helpless and so far away from the people she loved. A million miles from Claire and her mother. And from Will. She had no doubt that all of them were looking for her by now, but she'd been put in a box and buried underground for a reason. She wasn't meant to be found. Ever.

She'd conjured Will's voice because the imagined sound was her only comfort. Or maybe she really was starting to lose it. Dehydration could cause confusion, anxiety and, in extreme cases, hallucinations. Even now, with her eyes wide open and her lungs full of oxygen, she felt as if she could easily become untethered from reality and float off into an even darker place from which there would be no rescue or return.

What could be darker than the box?

"Death," she whispered.

But she wasn't dead yet and she needed to delay that finality for as long as she could. She still had work to do. Motives to ponder. Means and opportunities to explore. She flattened her hands against the lid as if she could physically push herself back down to reality.

"I'm okay," she said aloud. "I'm fine. I can keep going for as long as I need to. Do you hear me? For as long as I need to!"

Good! Then let's get back to work.

"I don't know where to start."

Yes, you do. You just don't want to go there.

"Go where?"

You need to think about James Ellis Ridgeway. It's time to deal with the Weatherman once and for all.

He was the last person Thora wanted to spend time with, especially inside the close confines of the box. Wasn't the seven years he'd lived inside her head long enough?

Don't look away, Thora. Keep digging.

There had to be a reason he'd come back into her life at this precise moment in time. In the course of one night out, Elise Barrett and Logan Neville had each mentioned his name in two separate conversations. True, people often wanted to talk about the Weatherman case if they knew of Thora's role in his capture, but two different people on the same night she'd been abducted? She wasn't a big believer in coincidences. If one looked hard and deep enough, a common thread could usually be unraveled. But if a thread existed that connected the Weatherman to Logan Neville and Elise Barrett, she'd yet to find it.

Doesn't mean it's not there. You said it yourself. Look harder and deeper.

She drew another long breath and once again committed herself to the investigation. She needed the distraction as much as she needed the truth, probably more so. But she was finding it difficult to concentrate. Water had become an obsession. She was no longer sweating and that was a very bad sign. What she wouldn't give at that moment for a single drop of moisture on her tongue. She tried to imagine herself in a rainstorm, tipping her head to the cool droplets as they splattered against her face. It didn't work. She was still trapped in the box and the walls were closing in on her.

Focus, Thora. You can do this.

She went back over the conversation with Elise Barrett, even speaking some of the remembered dialogue aloud. Far from grounding her in the familiarity of research and analysis, the sound of her own voice made reality seem far, far away.

Keep it together.

What floated to the surface from that conversation was Elise's speculation that she might have crossed paths with Ridgeway during one of his killing sprees. Rather than shuddering in dread at the prospect, she'd spoken of it in the same tone as if she were contemplating a chance meeting with a celebrity in an unexpected place. Maybe that wasn't so surprising. Elise Barrett wasn't the only one who had a fascination for the Weatherman. For a few months after his incarceration, devotees had gathered outside the prison walls hoping to catch a glimpse of him. The fixation was inexplicable to Thora, but then she'd not only studied Ridgeway for seven years, she'd also studied his victims. She could name all of them by heart. Two years after the case had been closed, the crime scene photos and videos still haunted her sleep.

She steadied her resolve and tried to remain alert. She needed to stay sharp in order to continue the investigation, but also to listen for outside noises, for even the faintest hint that rescue could be nearby. She might need to beat on the lid of the box and call up through the air pipe to get someone's attention. *Stay strong, stay vigilant. It's the only way you'll get through this.*

Funny how she now accepted the voice in her head as Will Dresden's. Or at least the Will Dresden she'd known thirteen years ago. His tone would have deepened with age and hardened with experience, but she would still know it anywhere. Even six feet under.

You can do this, Thora.

What if I can't? What if I'm not as strong as you think I am? I've got a breaking point.

You're not there yet.

How can you be so sure?

Because I know you. I know what you're capable of. Now brace yourself. We're not done yet with Ridgeway.

She had avoided concentrating on the brief conversation with Logan Neville because the revelation that her name had been mentioned in an interview with Ridgeway was far more unnerving than she wanted to admit. The thought of the killer obsessing over her role in his apprehension was downright scary. She knew what he was capable of, how he could manipulate, charm and coerce before revealing the monster inside. If the Weatherman was responsible for her incarceration, then God help her. There would be no getting out of this box. And the worst might be yet to come.

But she wasn't convinced of his involvement. Maybe she didn't want to believe it. Belfort, Texas, was a long way from his prison cell in Alabama. There was comfort in that distance. A false sense of security, perhaps. Coordinating a complicated abduction from behind bars wouldn't be easy when his every phone call, letter and visit had been monitored for the past two years. Maybe not every call. Cell phones were currency in prisons. Literally tons of the devices were found in sanitation systems every year. It seemed too coincidental that his name had been brought up to her just minutes before she'd been taken.

I don't want to do this, Will. I don't like letting a killer back into my life. It's dangerous.

I know. But you can't ignore him, and you can't assume anything at this point. You have to sift through every piece of evidence to get to the truth.

I'm tired. I just want to close my eyes and go to sleep.

You can't do that. Listen to me, Thora. You have to stay awake. You have to keep breathing. Do you hear me?

Yes, but your voice is starting to fade. You're too far away. I don't think you can make it in time.
I'll make it.
"Where are you, Will?"
Closer than you think. Just hold on.

Chapter Nine

As soon as Will got back to the station, he headed into the holding room to grill Noah Asher. As before, the reporter maintained his innocence and denied that he'd ever been inside Thora's townhouse until Will had caught him there earlier. He reiterated his conviction that James Ellis Ridgeway was somehow involved. The Weatherman was certainly clever enough to engineer a crime nearly four hundred miles away from his prison cell. He had the resources and he had an obsession with Thora. Will's every instinct warned him that Asher was playing him. He wasn't just the intrepid reporter he professed to be. The man was hiding something.

After the interview, he asked Detective Reyes to meet with him in his office. He'd assigned the seasoned investigator the task of tracking down Asher's contacts for two reasons. He trusted his former partner more than anyone else under his command and no one could dig up as much information in as short amount of time as Angel Reyes.

"The phone numbers he gave us checked out." He settled himself in the chair across from Will's desk and thumbed through his ever-present note-book. "His contacts weren't exactly thrilled to have a police detective from Belfort, Texas, in-terrupt their Saturday afternoon, and I can't say I blame them. We're hardly the big leagues. But after a little finessing, both his publisher and his literary agent corroborated Asher's credentials."

"That surprises me," Will admitted. "I half ex-pected you to come in here and tell me he made the whole thing up."

"He's legit, but he's not exactly in the big leagues, either. He has a book contract with a small press out of Mobile. They work with local authors and publish fewer than half a dozen titles a year. He also writes for a free weekly newspaper, but the bulk of his work seems to be digital. He's prolific online, but I have no idea how the guy makes a living. We're talking pieces for obscure blogs and fringe sites. His writing seems more of a hobby than a career. I haven't been able to dig up a single byline for a major publication and be-lieve me, I've looked. Over the past decade, he's written extensively about James Ellis Ridgeway, going all the way back to the first known kill out-side of Baton Rouge. He lives in a house owned by his mother, drives a ten-year old Camry and has a sister in Birmingham. Like Ridgeway, Asher seems to come up with enough funds from somewhere to live a modest but obsessive lifestyle." He glanced up from his notes. "My conclusion? He's one strange dude."

"That tracks with my impression of him," Will said.

"We can't hold him for much longer on a misdemeanor. If we cut him loose, we could put a tail on him."

"He suggested the same thing himself." Will thought about it for a moment, then nodded. "He's walking one way or another, so we may as well control his release."

"I'm on it."

"What about his podcast appearance? Were you able to corroborate the invitation from Logan Neville?"

"I've left a message but Neville hasn't returned my call. I've got his address. He lives in the Paseo District. If I don't hear back from him in the next half hour, I'll drive over to his place and have a chat with him in person."

Will fiddled with a pen. "That just leaves Ridgeway. We still need to verify Asher's trip to Donaldson Correctional Facility."

Reyes allowed himself a brief smile. "Saving the best for last, boss."

Will sat forward. "You found something?"

Reyes nodded. "In my experience, prisons are notoriously uncooperative and sometimes possessive of their inmates to a creepy degree. It can be unsettling. You have to present your request with the right amount of patience, deference and intimidation."

"Which you've mastered, I'm assuming."

"I had a lot of practice in El Paso. Some of my best confidential informants were on the inside." His phone dinged. He checked the text message, answered back and then stuffed the phone in his pocket. "Sorry about that. Okay, where was I? So after getting passed around a few times, I was finally connected to someone willing to check the visitors' log. Noah Asher saw Ridgeway two weeks ago just as he claimed. He signed in at nine o'clock on Tuesday, the fourteenth, for a noncontact visit. Signed out an hour later. But this is where it gets interesting." He paused for effect. "Asher neglected to mention that he's been making regular trips to the prison since Ridgeway's incarceration two years ago. He shows up like clockwork every second Tuesday of every month. Talk among the guards is that the two of them appear quite chummy."

"That's interesting, particularly since Asher seems intent on throwing Ridgeway under the bus. He keeps trying to convince me that Ridgeway is somehow behind Thora's abduction. I don't discount the possibility, but I also don't consider it a high probability."

"Well, this may change your mind," Reyes said. "Except for Ridgeway's attorney, Noah Asher has been his only visitor until the week before last when another name turned up on the visitors' log. This person signed in at ten and signed out at eleven. She would have just missed Asher."

"She? You've got a name?"

"I've got better than a name. I have a photograph of her signature." He handed Will his phone.

Will studied the shot of the log entry, then glanced up. "Thora went to see Ridgeway two weeks ago?"

"That's what someone wants us to think, but I checked her schedule. She had an eleven o'clock class that Tuesday. Plenty of witnesses saw her on campus. Whoever signed that log wasn't Thora Graham."

Will handed back the phone. "I'll need a copy of that signature." He fell silent as his mind raced. "Let's think about this for a minute. Anyone signing in at a maximum-security facility would have to show photo ID. Prisons have a lot of leeway on who they allow to visit and how often, but I'm guessing even a noncontact visit to a death row inmate would require a visitor request in advance."

"Which means Thora's kidnapping could have been in the works for weeks if not months," Reyes said. "And I seriously doubt it was planned and implemented by only one person."

"Agreed. I think we're looking for at least two suspects." Will leaned back in his chair, deep in thought. "As for the ID, it's not hard to get a passable fake. The tricky part would be getting a photo without Thora's knowledge."

"Why not just steal the original and return it before it's missed? Question is, why would someone go to so much trouble?"

"Maybe Thora was the only person Ridgeway would agree to see."

"Again, to what end?"

"I don't know," Will said in frustration. "Maybe whoever took Thora wants to use Ridgeway as a patsy. It's possible this whole thing is one big distraction. While we're wasting our time on Ridgeway, Thora's time is running out." He told himself to stay focused, but his mind kept straying back to that box. He pictured her inside, growing weaker and more desperate with each passing minute. By now, dehydration and heat exhaustion would be a problem. And that was assuming she didn't have any other injuries. That was in addition to her mental anguish. The notion that she had been put in that box because of a grudge against him was a devil on his shoulder he couldn't ignore.

Reyes pulled him back to the task at hand. "Maybe one of us needs to go talk to Ridgeway in person. I doubt he'll cooperate unless there's something in it for him, but you never know. He might let something slip."

"Guys like Ridgeway don't let things slip," Will

said. "He won't reveal anything he doesn't want us to know, but there are other ways of finding out the identity of his visitor. Call your contact at the prison and see if you can get surveillance footage from the visitors' area."

"I already checked. It's a no-go without a warrant."

"And warrants don't generally cross state lines," Will said. "I'll get the chief to make some calls. If he can get the feds on board, they can facilitate cooperation. Right now, I have something else I need you to do for me. What I'm about to request can't leave this room."

Reyes nodded. "No problem."

"Find out if Elise Barrett was on duty the day someone signed in as Thora at the prison."

Reyes stared at him silently for a moment, then nodded. "Anything else?"

"Report back to me and only to me as soon as you find out. I don't like asking you to do this. Digging into another cop's business is never pleasant. But if I start poking around, people will notice, and I don't want any gossip about this. I don't want anyone jumping to conclusions."

"Gotcha."

Will rose, drawing the meeting to a close just as his civilian assistant, Penny Yates, stuck her head in the door. "Sorry for the interruption."

"It's fine," Will said. "What's up?"

"There's a young lady at the front desk who

says she needs to talk to someone about Thora Graham. Says she's a student at the university. Under the circumstances, I didn't think we should keep her waiting."

Reyes pocketed his notebook and stood. "You want me to talk to her on my way out?"

"No, you've got other things to take care of." The two exchanged a glance. "I'll handle this."

"I'll bring her on back, then." Penny held the door for Reyes and the pair disappeared into the hallway. She returned a few minutes later with the student in tow.

"Deputy Chief Dresden, this is Baylee Fisher." She waited for the young woman to step inside the office and then pulled the door closed behind her.

Will motioned for the young woman to take a chair across from his desk. "I understand you're a student at the university."

"I'm a criminology major. If all goes as planned, I'll graduate next semester." She glanced around curiously, taking in the city map on the wall behind his desk and the framed citations scattered about the room. "You've received a lot of awards," she said in awe.

"Not all of them are mine. Most belong to the department." He waited until she was comfortably settled before giving her a prompt. "You have information about Thora Graham?"

She blinked at his brusqueness, then nodded.

"Yes, of course. We should get right to it. You're a busy man." She tore her gaze from the awards and gave him a tense smile. "Which is why I hope I'm not wasting your time. This may turn out to be nothing, but my instincts are usually pretty good. And I just knew I wouldn't be able to rest until I told someone what I heard."

Will sat back in his chair, outwardly relaxed as he tried to put her at ease. "Tell me what you know, and we'll decide where to go from there."

She nodded. "Professor Graham and I were supposed to meet in her office today. I showed up at nine on the dot, but her door was locked and she hadn't left a note. I thought she might be running late so I hung out in the library for a while and went back thirty minutes later. She still wasn't there. I checked the faculty parking garage and her space was empty. It's possible she forgot or something else came up, but I don't think so. I'm afraid something may have happened to her."

Will kept his tone neutral. "Why would you automatically assume something had happened to her?"

Her gaze was suddenly very direct. "Like I said, it's a feeling. An instinct. Plus, she looked kind of strange when I saw her at Molly's last night."

That got his attention. "You saw her at the pub? What time?"

"It was still early. Probably around ten or ten

thirty. She was just leaving when I caught her at the door."

"Was she alone?"

"Yes."

"You didn't see anyone walk out with her? Or behind her?"

She frowned in bewilderment. "No, and I'm sure I would have noticed."

"You said you caught her as she was leaving. I take it the two of you spoke?"

"For just a moment. I asked for a meeting and she said I could come by her office today." She wiped her hands down her jeans. "When I decided to come here, I didn't expect anyone to take my concerns seriously. Now all of a sudden, I find myself in the office of a deputy chief. All these questions about my interaction with Professor Graham last night can only mean one thing. Something *has* happened to her."

"Let's just stick to my questions for now," Will said. "How did she seem to you?"

Baylee gave him a knowing look. "I understand. You're keeping information close to the vest so that certain details can be used to trip up a suspect. I would do the same thing in your shoes."

"Then you won't mind answering my questions," Will said.

"Not at all. That's why I'm here. As to Professor Graham's behavior, she seemed a little…off, but not to the point where I thought she was inebriated or anything. I didn't think too much about it at the time, but I started to worry when she didn't show up today for our meeting. It's totally out of character for her."

"Did she say where she was headed last night?"

"No, but I assumed she was going home."

"Why did you want to meet with her today?" Will asked.

She leaned forward. "Can this stay between us?"

"That depends on what you have to say."

"It's just…" She clasped her hands in her lap. "You have to understand how it is on college campuses these days. If the wrong people were to get wind of my coming here, things could get very difficult for me. It only takes one post or video on social media to ruin your whole life."

"You came here because you wanted to do the right thing," Will reminded her.

She sighed. "I know."

"So tell me why you wanted to see Professor Graham. If I can keep the reason quiet, I will."

That seemed to satisfy her. "I'm taking a couple of summer classes so that I can graduate early. One under Professor Graham and the other under Professor Neville. I don't know if you're aware of Professor Neville's reputation, but it's very difficult to get into any of his classes. They fill up quickly, which makes it something of a Catch-22. If you want to be taken seriously as a criminology major, you not only have to take his classes, you also have to excel. He has favorites. The rest of us have to work twice as hard just to get a fair shake. One low test score or one wrong word from him and you're finished."

"I get it," Will said. "You don't want to get on his bad side."

"Yesterday, I left my notebook in his classroom. When I went back later to get it, I heard him arguing with someone. He mentioned Professor Graham. I didn't hear what he said, but the *way* he said her name stopped me dead in my tracks. I think he secretly resents her popularity. He's always been a big deal in the Criminology Department and then she comes in with her years of FBI experience and it makes his work seem trivial by comparison. Maybe that negative impression was already in my head when I heard him and I projected, but his tone didn't sound angry or bitter to me. I would describe it as ice-cold and diabolic."

"You didn't catch any of the conversation?"

"Just a bit when his voice rose. He said something like, *Don't you dare let me down.*"

Will lifted a brow at that. "That's pretty specific. Are you sure you heard correctly?"

"I may be paraphrasing but that's the gist of it."

"You didn't recognize the other voice?"

"Only that it was female. They were almost whispering, and I didn't want to get caught eavesdropping outside his door. Any one of his students would rat me out in a heartbeat just to get his nod of approval. I'd probably do the same if I were in their shoes. I ended up leaving without my notebook. But the tone of his voice stayed with me all day. It gave me a chill every time I thought about it. When I saw him talking to Professor Graham at the pub last night, I decided to warn her. Maybe what I overheard was something, maybe it was nothing, but I felt she needed to know."

"Why didn't you tell her last night if you thought it was that important?"

"I didn't want to be seen in a deep conversation with her or take the chance we'd be overheard. As I just explained, there's a lot at stake for me."

"How long did you stay at the pub after Professor Graham left?"

"Not that long. I think I left around eleven. It's really not my kind of place. I don't even drink. But Professor Neville invites his team to Molly's every Friday night and if I don't show up, I get left out of the planning. I'm already treated like a misfit. Sometimes I think the other members are just waiting for an excuse to kick me out."

"What kind of team are we talking about?" Will asked.

She sat a little straighter. "We investigate cold cases."

"You're amateur sleuths, in other words."

She didn't seem to care for his characterization. "You underestimate us. We don't get paid for our work, but I would hardly call us amateurs. We're all criminology majors. Most of us are just a semester or two away from doing what you do. One of us may even occupy this very office someday."

"More power to you," he said sincerely. "How many members are in this club?"

"We're a *team*," she stressed. "There are four of us, including Addison March. She's Professor Neville's TA."

Her expression altered almost infinitesimally when she mentioned the TA's name. Will watched her closely, noting the tension in her posture and the flicker of disapproval in her eyes.

"Could she have been the one you overheard in the classroom arguing with Professor Neville?" he asked.

She shrugged but her body language was hardly casual. "I wouldn't be surprised. She's certainly wormed her way into his good graces. And by good graces, I mean his bed. Everyone knows they're sleeping together."

"Not against the law," Will said.

"Though highly inappropriate. Needless to say, she receives preferential treatment. It's annoying that she gets the most interesting investigative assignments when there are smarter and more deserving members on Professor Neville's team."

"Like you?"

A frown flickered. "That's not for me to say."

"Let's go back to the conversation you overheard in his classroom. You said they spoke in a near whisper. How can you be so sure his companion was a woman?"

"I heard enough to recognize a female voice. Whether it was Addison or not, I don't know. There's an older woman who hangs out at the pub where we meet. I've seen her on campus a few times. I did wonder if it might have been her. Apparently, she and Professor Neville were involved for a time and I think she's still into him. She seems a little desperate for his attention."

Will was starting to get the bigger picture. Addison March and the desperate older woman weren't the only ones vying for Professor Neville's attention. "Was this woman at the pub last night?" he asked.

"Yes. I saw her talking to Professor Graham in the restroom. I think she's a cop. That's probably how she and Professor Neville met. I've heard him call her Elaine or Elise. Something that starts with an E."

Will said sharply, "Can you describe her?"

His curt tone seemed to catch her off guard. She stared at him wide-eyed for a moment before she answered. "Five seven, I would guess. Slender but fit. Blue eyes, curly red hair."

He strove to regain control of his outward reaction. Elise Barrett had deliberately misled him earlier about her interaction with Thora at the pub. Why lie about something so innocuous? "Are you sure you saw her with Thora Graham?"

"Yes, I'm positive. Is it important?"

"It might be. Did you see Professor Graham with anyone else last night?"

"Mostly she stayed with her group. As I said earlier, she spoke to Professor Neville for a few minutes at the table. Their conversation seemed friendly. I wouldn't have given it any thought if I hadn't overheard him mention her name earlier that day." She tucked her short hair behind her ears. "I understand you can't talk about an ongoing investigation, but can you at least tell me if Professor Graham is okay? She's not only my favorite instructor—she's been an inspiration ever since she came to U-SET."

"I'm sure she'll be gratified to hear that."

"I hope so. My dream is to work for the FBI. I want to hunt serial killers just like she did. Professor Neville doesn't think I have what it takes, but he's wrong."

Dead wrong? "I'm sure you'll do fine."

Will was about to rise and show her to the door when Penny popped her head back in. "Sorry for another interruption, but I thought you'd want to know." She held up her phone. "Tech just called. They've found something."

Will stood so quickly, his chair bumped back against the credenza. "Tell them I'm on my way."

Baylee rose more slowly. "She means the Technology Unit, right? Could I come with you? Whatever they're working on, I'm sure I could be of some help."

"Thanks for the offer, but I think we can manage. Penny?"

She nodded in understanding as she cut her gaze to Baylee. "I'll show you out."

Reluctantly, Baylee turned to follow her into the hallway. She paused at the doorway to glance back. "Good luck, Deputy Chief."

A FEW MINUTES LATER, Will stood staring at a series of stills from the second video the kidnapper had sent as one of the officers in the Tech Unit explained their discovery.

"When the camera pulled back from the air tube to reveal the forest…" The officer used the eraser end of a pencil to draw a pretend circle around the expanse on which he wanted Will to focus. "A tall, thin structure was captured in the distance rising above the treetops. The angle of the sun made it invisible until we isolated and enlarged the frame. Even then, we didn't know what we'd found. A cell tower seemed unlikely in such a densely wooded area."

Will studied the image. "Could it be the old fire tower? From what I remember of local history, it was built by the Forestry Service after World War II and abandoned sometime in the seventies. We used to hike out there when we were kids and climb to the top of that thing. You could see for miles."

The officer nodded appreciatively. "Good eye. That's exactly what it is. Once we made the identification, we could pinpoint the location using the recorded longitude and latitude. It's roughly ten miles north of the freeway, in the southernmost tip of a heavily wooded area that borders the Preserve. Using the tower as a landmark helped to narrow our search field, but we were still looking at acres and acres of deep forestland." He drew larger circles over the image.

Will noted the quiet excitement in his voice and glanced up from the frame. "I assume from your tone that you've found something else in the footage?"

"We did. Another marker here…" He pointed to a spot at the lower edge of a second still. "And here." He moved the pencil to the right. "When you put the two enlarged images together, you can see how the tower in the distance lines up dead center between the two artifacts."

"What are the artifacts?" Will asked.

"We think they're old gate columns. They may once have marked the entrance to a private road.

The rows of thick vegetation on either side indicate a fence line. Now look at the location of the columns in conjunction to the air tube." The third image was an enlarged still of the PVC pipe jutting from the ground, which the officer fitted between the other two frames like a puzzle piece. "When you watch the video, you don't notice the columns. The footage goes by too quickly and they're all but hidden by the congested growth. We only found them when we blew up the individual frames. But once spotted, we could tell the video was shot looking through those columns toward the air tube with the fire tower in the distance. See how everything is in alignment?" He traced a straight line from the center of the columns to the other two markers.

Will gave him a skeptical glance. "I'm still not convinced those are columns and even if they are, you don't think the positioning is a coincidence?"

"Virtually impossible. The orientation is too perfect. We think it's a map." He traced an X over the air tube.

Will tried not to jump ahead, but his adrenaline was already pulsing. "Just to be clear, you're saying the kidnapper planted a map of Thora's location in the video?"

"I'm saying the evidence is right here in front of us," the officer said. "What we don't know is why they'd leave such an obvious clue."

"I may have some idea. The map is only obvious if you're observant. In other words, someone without a keen eye and enough patience to go through the individual frames of the video could have easily overlooked one or all of the markers. The person or persons we're dealing with think they're smarter than the rest of us—or at least smarter than me. The text messages were provocative and condescending. They probably think they're still several steps ahead of us, but they underestimated you guys. They never expected you to find and identify the reference points so quickly."

The tech smirked and turned to fist-bump a colleague at the desk behind him.

"This is like a game to them," Will mused. "A deranged and dangerous contest."

The text messages had belittled his abilities and intellect in order to draw him into the investigation. For whatever reason, they wanted to pit their skills against his. If he couldn't find Thora in time, the hidden map in the video would be used to further disparage his competence. The guilt and second-guessing would eat him alive, which was almost certainly the intent. But why? He had a hard time imagining that someone from his past could be so dark and vindictive, but even the people you knew and trusted could be unpredictable.

Whatever the intent, he wouldn't allow himself to be caught in the trap of making it personal. He cleared his mind of self-doubt and any thoughts of retaliation as he studied the markers. He'd been born and raised in Belfort. He and his friends had roamed all through those woods as kids. If there'd been an old road with stone columns, they would surely have known about it.

Memories started to prod as he studied the frame.

"It's not a road," he said. "Not a road per se."

The officer glanced up from the screen. "What is it, then?"

Will tapped the image with his fingertip. "The columns mark the entrance to an old cemetery."

The officer looked startled by the revelation, then nodded excitedly. "That makes sense when you think about it. Easy to hide a new grave among the old ones."

"You wouldn't even have to disguise fresh digging," Will said. "The cemetery hasn't been active for decades. Most people probably don't even remember it's out there. I only know because my buddies and I came across it one day after we'd been to the fire tower. We were looking for an old house some kid told us about. Someone had supposedly been murdered inside and we wanted to see the bloodstains."

"Did you find it?"

"Yeah, finally, but we discovered the cemetery first. If memory serves, it's about three miles north of the tower. The area was so overgrown we didn't even realize we were walking over graves until we stumbled over pieces of broken headstones in the weeds. But I do remember a pair of columns and portions of a fence or wall. Back then, there was a wrought iron arch attached to the columns. I don't remember the name, but it may have been a private burial ground for the family who originally owned the property. This has to be the same cemetery."

The officer seemed intrigued by Will's recollection. "That's wild. I've lived here for nearly eight years, including college, and I've never even heard of the place. The county should have records, but that'll take time to comb through the deeds. Do you think you can find it from memory?"

Will thumped the screen. "We'll find it. We've got a map." He took out his phone and called Reyes. Once he'd briefed the detective on the discovery, he said, "Grab every available officer ASAP. The more boots on the ground the better. Even with a map, we've still got a lot of ground to cover."

"What about a warrant? Do we know who owns the property?"

"Exigent circumstances," Will replied.

"I'm more concerned about getting shot," Reyes countered.

"The place has been abandoned for years. We'll worry about finding the owner after we find her. We'll need shovels, ground-penetrating radar, a fiber-optic camera and anything else you can think of. Have an EMT team on standby. Let's go!"

Chapter Ten

Twenty minutes later, Will led the caravan with lights and sirens blasting down I-10 before exiting onto a two-lane county highway that took them deeper into the countryside. They made another right turn onto a dirt road that wound back east. A mile or so in, the road split. Will had to rely on memory to make the call. To the best of his recollection, the house was to the left and the cemetery to the right. The narrow trail that had once cut through the woods to the burial ground was long gone; the remnants of furrows now covered over with stands of evergreens and a thick carpet of brambles and underbrush.

Once the search party was in place, Will provided stills from the video that showed the alignment of the air tube with the columns and the distant fire tower. The image was fresh on everyone's mind as they fanned out in teams of two and began the slow trek through the woods. Eyes on the ground, they searched through dead leaves and tangled undergrowth looking for evidence of sunken graves and broken masonry.

All the while, Will had to beat back those stubborn doubts. What if he was wrong about the location? It had been years since he'd been out this way. What if the images from the video were deceiving? They could waste too much precious time searching in the wrong place.

Minutes passed and then an hour. And another hour. Sweat trickled down his back and soaked his shirt. Mosquitoes buzzed in his ears. It was nearing on five o'clock. Once the sun went down, the light would fade fast in the woods. They wouldn't have a prayer of finding the air tube after dark and by morning, it would be too late. *Thora, where are you? Where are you?*

"I found something!" an officer yelled.

Will's heart thudded as he turned. "What is it?"

"Looks like part of an old headstone."

Which meant they were at least in the right place. Or near the right place. Will let out a long breath of relief before he followed the sound of the officer's voice. As he approached, he spotted a second officer positioned between two crumbling stone pillars looking off toward the woods. The officer lifted an arm and used his finger to sight the fire tower in the distance. "The air tube should be straight ahead."

"Watch where you step," Will cautioned. They had no idea how shallow she might be buried or how flimsy the container. To an officer, they were eager for a rescue, but care had to be taken to avoid injury to the victim.

"Over here!"

By the time Will made his way through the columns, a loose circle had formed around a fresh burial site. The searchers parted, giving him a glimpse of the PVC pipe.

"We haven't heard any sounds coming from below," one of the officers said worriedly.

Will dropped to his knees and put his ear to the pipe. A sound echoed up through the tube. A rhythmic tapping…

"Shush. *Shush!*" He listened for a moment then said directly into the tube, "Thora? It's Will Dresden. Can you hear me?"

No answer.

A cold chill ran up his spine. What if they were too late? Or what if the kidnappers had already moved her? "Thora, please answer me!"

It seemed an eternity before a muffled voice came back to him. "Will?"

A smattering of cheers broke out at the sound of her voice. Then everyone fell into an awed silence. The gravity of the situation gripped them all. A woman had been buried alive just beneath their feet. It was only human nature to imagine themselves in her situation.

Will closed his eyes in relief. "I'm here, Thora."

"It's…really you this time?"

This time?

"Yes, it's me. Are you hurt?"

"I don't think so. I'm in some kind of box. Can you get me out?"

"Yes. Hang tight, okay? We'll have you out in no time."

Some of the officers had already started to dig. Will moved out of the way, watching, waiting and then taking his turn with a shovel. It was hard work, but no one minded. No one said anything, just quietly focused on the task at hand. When the first blade hit wood a few feet down, everyone scrambled to finish uncovering the container. The lid had been fastened in place. A crowbar was used to pry up the nails and then finally, *finally*, the top was carefully removed and Will got his first glimpse of Thora.

She lay on her back in the narrow container with her hands pressed to her sides. Her skin looked clammy; her eyes dazed by the light streaming down through the leaf canopy. Even though he'd heard her voice moments earlier, the terrible notion ran through his head that they really were too late.

His breath deserted him. He'd seen the video. He'd known what to expect. The image of her inside that box had run on repeat inside his head since early that morning. And yet the impact hit him as hard as any physical blow.

Applause and cheers erupted again as arms

reached down to help her. Will's was the first. She grasped his hand and he hauled her out of the box and up over the side of the hole they'd just dug. And then he held onto her while she regained her equilibrium. He held onto her far longer than she probably needed him to.

"Are you sure you're not hurt?" He looked her over. She still had on the clothes she'd worn to the pub last night. The soft blue top was wrinkled and dirty, her dark hair tangled with twigs. No blood that he could see. No obvious wounds, thank God.

"I'm okay." Her voice sounded croaky. "Dehydrated, I think. Overheated. A little dizzy." She sat down abruptly on the mound of dirt at the edge of the hole. "Can I have some water?"

An officer handed Will a bottle. He twisted off the cap and knelt in front of Thora, observing the ashen tint to her skin as he gave her the water.

"Thank you." She lifted the bottle and drank deeply.

"Take it easy," he said. "Not too much too soon."

She nodded and took a smaller sip before handing back the bottle.

"The EMTs are on the way," he told her. "Just rest until we can get a stretcher out here."

She glanced at the now empty box and shivered. "I don't need a stretcher. I can walk."

"I don't think that's a good idea. It's at least a

quarter mile back to the road and you seem a little unsteady on your feet."

"I'll be all right in a minute." Instead of turning her back on the box, she sat facing it. "How long was I down there?"

The shock of what she'd been through hit Will anew with that question, but he managed to cover his reaction. "We think you were taken sometime around ten last evening. It's five o'clock in the afternoon of the following day. Saturday. Roughly nineteen hours."

She let out a breath. "I couldn't tell. It was dark in the box. I lost track of time. Nineteen hours isn't so long."

"It must have seemed like an eternity."

She nodded. "The heat was pretty intense. I was given a little water through the tube but that was hours ago."

He latched onto her revelation. "One of the kidnappers was out here today?"

"Someone was. Early morning if I had to guess because the box got a lot hotter as time wore on."

Will tore his gaze from Thora and focused his attention on the container. It looked to be made of pine plywood, a material light enough to be carried through the woods without much trouble by two fit adults. The lid had been constructed to rest snuggly over the top and had been hammered in place at the corners. A hole had been drilled at one end to accommodate the air tube, which had been fixed in place with a ring of silicon. The box was incredibly narrow. Thora wouldn't have been able to stretch her arms and legs, much less roll to a new position. She'd had to lie flat on her back in pitch blackness for nineteen hours, not knowing where she was or if anyone would find her in time. Will could only imagine the things that had gone through her head, the struggle she must have fought to keep her sanity. Under the circumstances, she seemed miraculously calm and steady.

As to the grave, he judged the depth at around four feet. Probably dug well in advance and out-fitted with the container before Thora had been kidnapped.

"It was built for me, wasn't it?" She was still staring at the open box. "The size is custom."

"All we know for sure is that it was built for someone your size or smaller."

Her gaze met his. "Do you know who put me in there?"

"Not yet. We believe we're looking for multiple suspects. We were hoping you could help us identify at least one of them."

She shook her head. "I never saw the person who grabbed me. I'm certain I was drugged. I think someone spiked my drink in the pub. I felt light-headed before I left. Then I remember bright lights in my eyes and someone telling me not to fight. I was shoved in the back of a vehicle and then the next thing I knew, I woke up in the box."

The terror she must have felt in that moment… Will swallowed and kept his tone even. "You didn't recognize the person's voice?"

"They used a voice changer. Or maybe that's just the way I remember it. The parking lot was spinning by that time. I'd taken out my phone to call Claire when the lights blinded me…" She wrinkled her brow in concentration. "That's it, I think. That's all I remember."

"Don't try to force it," Will said. "Something else may come back to you later."

She nodded before turning to scour their surroundings. After the sound of clanging shovels and human effort, the forest had grown quiet again. All activity had ceased as soon as Thora had been freed from the box. Now the officers stood back respectfully to allow her some privacy, but Will had a feeling they were hanging on her every word. The tableau seemed surreal. More than a decade had passed since he'd last spoken to Thora Graham and there they sat at the edge of her would-be grave.

It was still hot out and hundreds of mosquitoes were swarming. He swatted one from her hair, but she hardly noticed. She seemed a little dazed and slightly in awe of the landscape. She ran a hand up her arm and shuddered. "Where are we? It looks like we're in the middle of nowhere."

"We're about twelve or thirteen miles north of I-10. The old fire tower is just south of here." He paused. "If you look over your shoulder…" He pointed toward the thick row of vegetation behind them. "You can make out a pair of stone columns rising up through the vines and shrubs. Believe it or not, that's how we were able to find you. It won't make a lot of sense without the video for context, but from a certain angle, the air tube they put in the box lines up perfectly with the columns and the fire tower."

She drew her knees up and wrapped her arms around her legs. The position seemed poignantly protective to Will. "What video?"

"I was texted two videos early this morning. One of you inside the box and an external shot of the air tube sticking up from the ground. The camera panned wide from the tube to show the density of the surrounding woods. It was meant to make us feel that searching for where they buried you would be like looking for a needle in a haystack. And it did seem that way until Tech discovered landmarks in the footage."

She stared at him in confusion. "That all sounds…elaborate."

"It's definitely one for the books," he agreed.

A light breeze blew down through the trees and she tipped her face, eyes closed as the wind ruffled her hair. Will studied her profile. She was dirty, pale and haggard, but she'd never looked more beautiful to him.

She caught him staring at her. "You said the fire tower is just south of here?"

"Yes, that's right. We're at the edge of the Preserve."

"Then I think I know where we are." Her voice turned slight accusing. "You didn't want to tell me, did you?"

Now Will was confused. "Tell you what?"

"They buried me in an old cemetery."

He stared at her in surprise. "How could you possibly know that? You can't see the graves or the headstones without tramping through the weeds looking for them. Did you regain consciousness at any point after you were taken? Did you hear someone mention the location?"

She shook her head. "I woke up in the box."

"Then how did you know about the cemetery?"

She glanced over her shoulder toward the columns. "You told me about it once." When he continued to stare at her blankly, she said, "Don't you remember? You and some of the other boys in the neighborhood discovered it one day when you were hiking in the woods. There's an old house around here somewhere. You said it was haunted. You took pictures because you thought I wouldn't believe you."

"I told you about this place?" He shook his head. "I guess it made more of an impression than I remembered. I must have filed it away in my subconscious. Do you still have those photographs?"

"Maybe at my mom's house. I could look through my old photo albums if it's important."

"It might be. I'm curious how the kidnappers knew the cemetery was here."

"Maybe one of them grew up in the area. Or maybe you told someone else, and they also filed it away in their subconscious."

Which only bolstered the theory that at least one of the kidnappers was someone he knew, someone with a deep-seated grudge against him.

Thora took the water bottle from his hand and sipped slowly.

Reyes walked over, and Will rose. "Did you find anything?"

"Not yet. If there's any trace evidence that hasn't been contaminated by the digging, we need to protect it until CSU can sweep the area for DNA and fiber samples. It'll be a miracle if anything can be recovered, but you never know. Sometimes all it takes is a partial print." He glanced down at Thora. "I'm Detective Reyes. You have no idea how happy we are to see you."

"Almost as happy as I am to see you," she said.

He smiled. "I bet."

"ETA on the paramedics?" Will asked.

Reyes reluctantly tore his gaze from Thora. "Ten minutes. They made a wrong turn."

"You're kidding me."

"GPS can only help so much when you're this far off the beaten track." He glanced around. "How do you think the kidnappers even found this place?"

"We were just wondering the same thing. I knew about the cemetery as a kid. Maybe one of them did, too."

"I've been thinking about that map," Reyes said. "If they wanted us to find her, what was the point of all this?" He motioned to the box.

Will moved a few steps away from Thora and lowered his voice. "I'm guessing they didn't expect us to find her so quickly. Not until after her time ran out."

Reyes muttered an expletive, which mirrored Will's sentiments.

"Someone was here this morning," he said. "They brought her water. We need to comb these woods. Look for plastic bottles, drink cans, food wrappers. Anything we can lift a print from. They must have made a few trips out here getting everything ready before they took her. If something got left behind, we need to find it."

Reyes nodded. "Already on it, Boss."

Will moved back to Thora. "How are you holding up?"

"How far did you say the road is from here?"

"Quarter of a mile, maybe less." He hunkered beside her once more. "Why?"

"I don't want to wait for the paramedics. I'm starting to feel—" She tucked back her hair with a trembling hand as her voice lowered to a pleading whisper. "I need to get out of these woods. Will—"

He took one look at her panicked expression and nodded. "Come on. We'll head back toward the road together." He took her hand and drew her to her feet.

For a moment, she looked on the verge of losing it. *And who could blame her?* Then she took a steadying breath and nodded. "I'm okay."

He kept a hand on her arm as he nodded to Reyes. "We'll meet the EMTs at the road."

Reyes gave him a questioning look before he returned the nod.

"No one except CSU gets back here," Will said. "We need to station a couple of officers out on the road in case any reporters or onlookers get wind of this."

"No worries, I'm on it."

They were well away from the scene before Thora stopped and turned to him. The scent of pine permeated the warm air, and he could hear an owl in the distance. The dreamlike feeling persisted. "What's wrong?"

"I just wanted to thank you for not making me wait back there. I was okay when I first got out of the box." She glanced away. "I thought, 'I did it. I actually made it through to the other side and I'm perfectly fine.' And then…"

"Shock set in. It happens."

She hugged her middle. "Maybe I'm not as strong as I've always wanted to believe."

"Do you think any one of us could have handled it better? Back there, when you talked about waking up in the box…" Words failed him. He swallowed past a sudden tightness in his throat. "I can't begin to imagine what that must have been like."

Her eyes took on a faraway look as if she were reliving the moment. "What happens now?"

He didn't know if her question was literal or metaphorical. He answered in a matter-of-fact way. "Once we get to the road, I'll call ahead so your mom and sister can meet you at the hospital."

When he would have moved forward, she took hold of his arm and held him back. "Thank you, Will. Thank you for finding me."

"You don't need to keep thanking me. I'm just sorry it took us as long as it did."

Her eyes looked dark and luminescent in the light that spangled down through the trees. Now it was Will who shivered.

"It doesn't matter," she said. "I knew you'd come."

WILL WATCHED THE ambulance as it turned and headed back toward the highway with Thora safely tucked inside. A cloud of dust followed in the vehicle's wake. He'd resisted the temptation to crawl in the back and see her safely to the ER, but there was still work to be done out here. Besides, it wasn't his place to go with her. Hadn't he vowed earlier not to make this personal? A difficult task when the kidnappers seemed to be goading him at every turn.

He could hear shouts from the woods as officers combed through the underbrush and the CSU team processed the box and immediate burial area. Once they'd swept for fibers and DNA, the grave would be covered with a tarp and the box would be transported to the station where it would be logged into evidence.

Despite the activity, he didn't immediately return to the site. The men under his command needed to know that he trusted them to get the job done without looking over their shoulders or second-guessing their decisions. Instead, he decided to scout a wider area. If the house still stood, he decided it might be worth his time to take a look around the property. Probably a long shot, but if the kidnappers knew about the graveyard, they may also have known about the old homestead.

He searched along the ditches for a few hundred feet and then doubled back to the split in the road. Turning left this time, he followed what remained of a narrow lane until he caught a glimpse of the house through the trees. He approached cautiously on the slim chance that someone might be hiding inside.

Weeds and brambles had taken over the once spacious front yard. The thorny tendrils clutched at his ankles, making him thankful for his leather boots and denim jeans. The vegetation was flattened in places as if a vehicle had recently been driven back that way. Probably hunters looking for javelinas or hikers searching for a shortcut into the Preserve. Or someone scouting a meth lab location. Whatever the case, the proximity to the cemetery triggered Will's curiosity. Taking out his phone, he called Reyes to alert him of the find.

Once Will had reported his position and described his surroundings, Reyes said, "Want me to meet you there?"

"Not yet. Let me poke around first. No need to waste your time and mine on a wild-goose chase. I'll call if I need you."

Will slid the phone back in his pocket and set out across the property. Honeysuckle grew in tangled thickets and as the sun sank beneath the treetops, the sticky scent thickened. Mosquitos swarmed, drawn by his body heat and the carbon dioxide he emitted. Once he was past a sentry of live oaks, he got his first unimpeded look at the house.

The structure was in a lot worse shape than he remembered. The wraparound porch sagged badly in places and portions of the peaked roof had collapsed beneath the weight of the kudzu creeping over the shingles. Most of the windows were broken from what he could see, and the overgrown yard was littered with tires, rusty appliances and an old box spring. The place had obviously been used as a dumping ground over the years, which could explain the flattened weeds he'd noticed earlier at the edge of the yard.

As he stood gazing up at the two-story facade, memories of that first visit came back to him. His friends had run across the yard and up the wobbly steps to the porch while Will had hung back, both fascinated and repelled by the house. Even now he felt the tug of those warring emotions—a strange sense of melancholy that mingled with the innate creepiness of the place. He hadn't gone inside that day with his friends and he could never explain why, even to himself. They'd come out a little while later with gruesome tales of blood splattered walls and piles of old bones, none of which Will had believed. Or so he'd told himself. Maybe his inexplicable skittishness was why he'd put the house and the neighboring cemetery out of his mind for so many years. Maybe he just didn't like abandoned places.

He stood at the bottom of the porch steps and texted Reyes once again:

Going inside. Floorboards and roof look iffy. If you don't hear back, send help. He was only half kidding.

Reyes texted back: Watch out for copper-heads.

Snakes were the least of his worries, Will decided as he put away his phone. He wasn't embarrassed to admit the place still spooked him. Which was foolish. He didn't believe in the dead coming back and he wasn't afraid of the living. He was armed, trained and experienced. If anyone had driven back here to conduct nefarious business, he could deal with the situation. Besides, the sirens would have already scared them away. His trepidation wasn't rational and so he shook off the disquiet and tramped through the waist-high weeds to the house.

Before climbing the porch steps, he decided to do a perimeter check, taking note of the space beneath the house where any number of critters might hide and an old shed in the back where something larger might skulk. Then he returned to the front and tested those rickety steps, taking care not to put a foot through the rotting porch. A screen door hung on one hinge. He pulled it back and peered inside. He had no reason to believe anyone was around, but he still felt the need to call out. "Hello?"

The greeting echoed through the empty rooms and bounced back out to him. He stepped inside and moved gingerly across the creaking floorboards to stand in the center of the room. Vines growing through the broken windows filtered the late afternoon sunlight, casting gloom throughout the interior. Cobwebs hung in thick drapes from shadowy corners. The only furniture left behind was a wooden table and a couple of broken chairs. The bare floor was littered with moldy books, old clothing and clumps of what looked to be animal fur. The musky odor of vermin permeated the air, the foul scent punctuated by the rustle of claws across the floor and in the walls.

It was not a pleasant place, though there were no blood splatters on the walls or piles of human bones as previously claimed by a pair of mischievous twelve-year-old boys.

As Will became accustomed to the gloom, he slid his gaze slowly over the walls and ceiling and finally back across the floor where a recent visitor had left footprints in the dust. Adrenaline started to pump as he tracked the prints from the front room, through the kitchen and out to the back porch. The trail ended at the top of the steps.

His scalp prickled a warning as he stood there listening to the countryside. *You should have waited for Reyes.*

Too late now.

He ran fingers through his hair, dislodging cobwebs as he told himself he was letting his imagination get the better of him. Was it any wonder? He and his team had just dug up a woman who had been buried alive in an old cemetery. Someone who had once meant everything to him. He had a right to be a little jumpy, particularly with all the recent talk about the Weatherman. The serial killer had spent a decade traveling back and forth across the country, leaving a trail of victims in his wake. This place was only a few miles from the interstate. The perfect dumping ground for the bodies that had yet to be found.

At that very moment, James Ellis Ridgeway was sitting on death row in an Alabama prison. Irrational to think he'd somehow had a hand in Thora's abduction, much less that he'd stumbled across this property during one of his killing sprees. Foolish to think that his evil lingered. Yet there was something about this place...

Will wanted to laugh at himself—a seasoned law enforcement officer letting his imagination and an abandoned house creep him out—but he'd learned a long time ago that listening to his instincts usually paid off. He stood on the porch, watching and waiting as the sun slipped lower and the air finally started to cool. He could already hear the eerie yip of a coyote in the distance. A flock of blackbirds rose suddenly from the treetops, the flapping wings physically startling him. He rested his hand on the handle of his holstered weapon as he continued to observe his surroundings. A shadow moved at the side of the outbuilding. For a moment, Will could have sworn someone stood in deep shade watching him. Common sense told him it was nothing more than a bush or tree limb stirred by a faint breeze.

Still, he unfastened the catch on his holster as he went down the steps and walked through the weeds to the building. Scouring his surroundings, he slid back the barrel lock and propped the door open with a block of wood. The interior was dark, save for the light streaming in through the open door. On the opposite wall, a single window had been covered with a cloth or tarp, blocking the natural light from the west.

Will hovered in the doorway until his eyes once again grew accustomed to the gloom. The shed must once have been used as a workshop. Long tables built of plywood and two-by-fours lined rough-hewn walls where rusty tools still hung from pegs.

Like the house, the shed smelled of nesting rodents and damp earth, but beneath those fusty odors, he caught a whiff of something that might have been fresh sawdust. Unlikely. There was no power to the house or shed and judging by the condition of the hand tools, no one had touched them in decades.

As he stepped inside, he realized what he had mistaken as another worktable or bench was, in fact, a coffin-sized box. A thrill skirted up his spine. The container looked very much like the one in which Thora had been trapped. He estimated the size to be a few inches longer and wider than hers, just large enough to accommodate a lean adult male roughly his size.

A hole had been cut at one end and fitted with a piece of PVC pipe. The lid rested on the box but wasn't yet secured. He presumed that meant the box was empty, but even as he reached for the top, he heard something that might have been fingernails scrape against the wood. Bracing himself for what he'd find, he shoved the lid aside.

The light from the doorway didn't reach far enough to penetrate the interior of the box. He couldn't immediately see what had been trapped inside until the rat scurried to the opposite end and cowered in a corner.

Will had no idea whether the rodent had been purposefully imprisoned or had slithered down the PVC pipe and couldn't find a way out. The former would suggest someone had been inside the shed recently. Perhaps only hours ago. Perhaps only minutes ago. While he watched, the rat found enough courage to scurry up the wall of the box and disappear over the side.

He removed a pair of latex gloves from his pocket and began a methodical search of the space. Whoever had built that box and transported it all the way out to the shed must surely have left something behind in the process.

Circling the room slowly, he took in the details he'd overlooked in his initial search. The cobwebs had been knocked down from the corners and the wooden floorboards looked to have been recently swept. The worktables had also been cleared of debris. He wondered when and why the box had been left in the shed.

He took out his phone, using the flashlight beam to play over the rough walls and ceiling and then he crouched to shine the light up under the worktables. Something metallic gleamed on the floor. Remembering the latchkey beneath Thora's car, he reached under the table with his gloved hand. Nothing but a nail. The floorboards were rotting through in places. Probably dozens of loose nails scattered about the place. But the one in his hand wasn't as worn as he would have expected in a place this old and leaky.

Pushing the table aside, he took a closer look at the floor. The nail heads on several of the boards looked new. He found a claw hammer to pry up the planks and then angled his beam down into the opening. A human skull grinned up at him.

Chapter Eleven

"Judging by the size of skull, we're looking at the remains of a child or a very small adult," Reyes said a little while later as he and Will hunkered beside the opening he'd created in the floor. "Hopefully, the DNA database can give us a match."

"That could take a while." Will was still shaken by the discovery. Even with the shed door propped open and several officers milling about outside, he felt a chill up and down his spine. There were things even the most experienced law enforcement officers never got used to, crimes against children being at the top of the list.

Reyes shifted his weight to his other foot. "Medical examiner is on the way. Maybe she can give us some idea of how long the bones have been down there."

"Dr. Larkin is good, but we may need to consult with a forensic anthropologist. Skeletal remains are tricky."

Reyes nodded. "I'll call Dr. Grover at Texas State, but I doubt he can fit us into his schedule before late next week. And that's being optimistic."

"The exhumation can't wait that long. Look at the size of the skull, Angel." Will's voice turned grim. "That's not a small adult. The victim was a child. I don't want to leave the remains unprotected any longer than necessary."

"I hear you."

They were both silent for a moment.

"You grew up in the area," Reyes said. "You've been on the force for a long time. Any idea who the victim might be?"

"I keep thinking about a kid that went missing ten years ago while walking home from school. Despite an intensive search, his body was never found. He was nine years old. The size of the skull looks about right."

"A decade is a long time for a family to remain in limbo," Reyes said. "What was the boy's name?"

"Danny Hagan. Only child, troubled home. Stepfather heavily into drugs. The guy looked guilty as hell. An eyewitness claimed they saw Danny get into his truck, but we never found enough evidence to charge him."

"You worked the case?"

"Elise Barrett and I did some legwork as first-year detectives. We beat the bushes for months. Never found so much as a trace. A child goes missing in broad daylight...that's the kind of case you don't forget. The kind that keeps you up at night a decade later."

"We've all got those," Reyes muttered.

"The lead investigator was a guy named Pennington. He retired a few years back."

Reyes glanced up. "Barrett's name sure seems to be popping up a lot lately."

Too often for comfort in Will's book. "Did you have time to get the information we talked about earlier?"

"Yeah, and you're not going to like it. She took two vacation days at the beginning of the week in question. Doesn't mean she hopped a plane to Alabama. Could be she just wanted a long weekend."

"But we now know it's a possibility." Will rested his forearm across the top of his thigh. Reyes was right. The new information didn't sit well. He didn't like questioning a fellow officer's integrity, much less someone with whom he'd once been involved. But ever since he'd spoken to Elise earlier that day, doubt had continued to niggle.

Reyes narrowed his gaze. "What's going on with Barrett? I'm sure you have your reasons for digging into her whereabouts, but if any of this is personal—"

"It's not," Will assured him. "She was at the pub last night. I asked her if she'd spoken to Thora and she lied to my face. They were seen having a conversation. I don't know why she tried to deceive me about something that could be easily verified, but now I can't help wondering what else she may have lied about. Or what she might be hiding."

Reyes glanced at him. "I couldn't help noticing earlier your interaction with Thora. Feel free to tell me it's none of my business and we'll move on."

"Everything about the investigation is your business. Thora and I grew up together. We were best friends as kids and we dated all through high school. Things got a lot more serious in college. I wanted to marry her."

"What happened?"

"It's a long story and this isn't the time or place," Will said.

"I only ask because of the reference to her in the text messages. The sender called her your precious Thora. Sounds like something a jealous ex might write."

"That's one of the reasons I went to see Elise. I kept telling myself no way she could ever be involved in a kidnapping, much less burying someone alive. She's a cop, for God's sake. But then she lied to me. For whatever reason, she didn't want me to know she'd spoken to Thora last night."

"Maybe you should ask Thora what they talked about."

"Oh, I intend to. Just as soon as we're finished here."

They both returned their attention to the bones.

"You know what I think?" Reyes asked.

"I'm almost afraid to ask."

"We know the Weatherman was active as far back as ten years. The body of the first known victim was found a few miles off I-10 near Baton Rouge in an abandoned property not unlike this place."

"You think Ridgeway did this?" Will glanced around at their surroundings as his uneasiness deepened. "You're letting Noah Asher get in your head. Most of Ridgeway's victims were adult females."

"Most but not all. He started with children."

"It's a long shot," Will insisted.

"Maybe, maybe not. The FBI always believed Ridgeway held back the names and burial locations of some of his victims as bargaining chips. Let's think about this for a minute. We know Asher has been visiting Ridgeway every month for the past two years, but what we don't know is whether or not they had a relationship before Ridgeway was incarcerated. Asher claims he came to town to do a podcast as PR for an upcoming book about the Weatherman. You caught him red-handed in Thora Graham's home and we know he kept tabs on her right before she was taken. He also claims Ridgeway has a fascination for Thora, but it seems to me they both do. What if Ridgeway told him where the body was buried?"

"You think he came out here, pried up the planks to view the remains and then nailed the floor back down? Why?"

"Timing." Reyes swatted a mosquito from his face. "What better way to get your book noticed than to discover the skeletal remains of one of the Weatherman's first victims? A child, no less. You have to admit the PR from those headlines would beat the hell out of a podcast."

"He said he came to town because Logan Neville would only do the interview in person."

"Asher said a lot of things. Conveniently, we haven't been able to corroborate that part of his story with Professor Neville."

Will pondered the possibility for a moment. "Let's assume everything you say is true. How would he explain his discovery? You don't just drive across three states and happen upon human remains buried beneath the floorboards of an abandoned shed out in the middle of nowhere."

"He could basically tell the truth. Ridgeway told him where he'd hidden the boy's body and Asher wanted to make certain the claim was true before he got the family's hopes up."

"Then why kidnap Thora?"

"They struck a bargain. Asher gets the story of a lifetime and Ridgeway gets payback for Thora's part in his capture."

"It's an interesting theory," Will said. "But how do you explain the second box?"

"I haven't worked that part out yet," Reyes admitted. "Whoever left it here must have a connection to the skeletal remains...unless we're dealing with one hell of a coincidence." He paused for a moment. "But let's go with that angle for a minute. Say the kidnappers stumbled across the bones by accident. The discovery was made while they were planning or initiating the abduction. They'd have no choice but to nail the floor back in place and remain silent about the remains."

Will nodded toward the wooden container. "So who do you think the second box was meant for?"

Reyes shrugged. "That's the big question. Maybe you were right earlier. Maybe all this business with the Weatherman is nothing more than a false lead. A red herring."

"I don't know what to think at this point," Will admitted. "All I know right now is that nothing makes sense and everything seems connected."

"Early days," Reyes said. "We'll figure it out."

He rose and went outside to meet the medical examiner, leaving Will alone once more in the shed. He rubbed the back of his neck as he stared down at the skull. The empty eye sockets stared back at him accusingly. *What took you so long?*

THE EMTs HAD hooked Thora up to an intravenous drip and checked her vitals on the way to the hospital. Upon arrival, she was whisked into an emergency room cubicle where a forensic nurse drew blood, bagged her clothing and personal effects and collected trace evidence from her skin, hair and beneath her fingernails. Afterward, she was allowed to shower and wash the dirt and twigs from her hair before a doctor came in to conduct a more thorough examination. The dehydration was severe enough to warrant an overnight IV so a few hours after her arrival, she was moved to a private room on an upper level of the hospital.

The adrenaline rush from the rescue had kept her going throughout the necessary procedures. She'd coped well enough until she was left alone while her mother and sister underwent the required screening process for visitors. The quiet was nice at first. Gave her a moment to catch her breath. She was on the fifth floor, too high to see anything more than the glow of streetlights below, but she had a perfect view of the rising moon. At any other time, she might have taken no notice, but after being trapped in a buried box, she found the night sky surreal and impossibly beautiful. In those hushed moments with nothing to distract her, she felt almost at peace. Then without warning, terror descended. Her heart started pounding and she found herself shaking so hard she had to grip the edges of the mattress.

By the time her mother and sister walked through the door, she'd managed to talk herself down enough to greet them with a smile. Her mother immediately began to fret about her color and fuss with the bed covers.

"Mom, I'm fine. I've been examined and given a clean bill of health except for dehydration, which is what this is for." She lifted her hand with the IV needle. "By tomorrow morning, I'll be as good as new. I already feel a lot better."

"You just look so frail lying in that bed."

"I'm the opposite of frail," Thora said. "I was raised by you, wasn't I?"

Maddie bit her lip. "You're strong despite me, I think."

"Please, both of you just stop." Claire moved around to the window side of the bed. She'd taken the time to style her hair and apply makeup before leaving the house, but in the harsh hospital lighting, Thora could detect worry lines across her forehead and a faint darkness beneath her eyes.

"Stop what?" she asked with a frown.

"This whole back-and-forth you have going on. Mom acting as though you're still ten and you pretending you're fine like you always do. But you're not fine. You were kidnapped and buried alive, for God's sake. I don't care how much experience and training you've had—you don't come through something like that unscathed."

"I never said I was unscathed," Thora said. "Physically, I'm unharmed."

Claire barreled on without the slightest hesitation or hint of self-awareness. "It's almost an insult to shut us down like that. We're allowed to worry. Do you have any idea what we went through? We didn't know if we'd ever see you again. Or if we'd even be able to find your body. You can't imagine the things that went through my head."

"Oh, I think I can," Thora murmured.

"Mom, stop hovering. You'll drive us both up the wall. And you—" Claire trained her gaze on Thora. "Stop trying to sweep your emotions under the rug. You need to let us in this time."

"Claire," Maddie said from the other side of Thora's bed. "Shut up."

She looked dumbfounded. "What?"

"You heard me, dear. You know I love you and I would do anything for you, but this isn't about you. We've got our Thora back. We need a moment to appreciate how lucky we are. Yes, I'm guilty of hovering and I sometimes let the negative emotions get the better of me, but your bullying doesn't help any of us right now. Just let Thora be. We'll have plenty of time as a family to process what happened. She's safe and nothing else matters."

Claire opened her mouth to retort, then clamped her lips shut when someone knocked on the door. Or maybe when she glimpsed the stubborn set of Maddie's jaw. Thora couldn't help but be amused by the unexpected dynamic. Her sister was accustomed to steamrolling over everyone and everything in her path. She didn't know how to react when someone pushed back, especially their normally docile and sometimes absentminded mother.

They all turned toward the door as Will came into the room. Thora was glad they'd had a few moments alone together in the woods. She was better prepared to conceal her emotions in his presence.

He looked a little taken aback by the trio of curious gazes. Despite the awkwardness, his focus went straight to Thora. She stared back until embarrassment and uncertainty prompted her to glance away. She wondered if anyone else had noticed the shift in energy. The almost palpable tension that suddenly pulsed through the room. Thirteen years and a dead husband, and Will Dresden still had the power to make her heart flutter.

"Sorry for the interruption." He waited inside the door. "I just came by to see how you're doing tonight."

She forced a smile. "Much better. They let me shower and brush my teeth. I feel like a new person."

Claire muttered something under her breath as she filled a water cup.

Thora tried to ignore her sister's touchiness. "One of the orderlies said the police had requested

I be moved to a private room near the nurse's station. Was that your doing?"

"It's protocol when we have cause to worry about a continued threat. The ER has too many people coming in and out at all hours, especially on a Saturday night. It'll be easier to spot someone up here who doesn't belong."

Maddie said in alarm, "What do you mean a continued threat? You don't think the person who took Thora will come back, do you?"

Thora met Will's gaze and shook her head slightly.

He said, "It's a precaution. I'm putting a guard outside the room for the rest of the evening and night. You don't need to worry. She'll be in good hands."

"A guard?" Maddie looked stricken. "That's more than a precaution. It sounds like you're expecting trouble." She wrung her hands. "I thought the nightmare was over when you found Thora unharmed."

"How can it be over when the kidnapper hasn't been caught?" Claire pinned Will with a glare. "You must have a lead by now."

Thora silently counted to ten, then said, "Will you both please relax? Nothing is going to happen to me while I'm in the hospital. And I'm certain Will and his team are doing everything in their power to identify and locate the unsub. The best thing we can do is stay out of their way."

The conversation had deflated Maddie's moment of positivity. She looked tense and unhappy, which, perversely, seemed to buoy Claire's spirits. She came around the bed and patted Maddie's arm. "I don't know about you, but now that my nerves have finally settled, I could do with a bite to eat." She motioned to Will as she moved toward the door. "Can I have a word before we go?"

Thora wondered what that was all about. For her mother's sake, she tried not to look concerned as the pair stepped into the hallway and closed the door.

They returned a few minutes later and Claire beckoned to their mother from the doorway. Maddie leaned down and kissed Thora's forehead before she reluctantly joined her other daughter in the hallway. To Will, she said, "You'll keep her safe?"

"You have my word."

And then they were gone, and Thora found herself alone in the room with the man she'd said goodbye to thirteen years ago. She thought about the imaginary conversations she'd had with him before her rescue and wondered what he would say if she told him that he'd saved her life and her sanity before he'd physically found her. The box had been a nightmarish prison and his voice in her head had been her lifeline.

She couldn't take her gaze off him as he moved

to the foot of the bed. He somehow seemed different and exactly the same. "What was that about?"

"You mean Claire? She wanted to follow up on a matter we spoke about this morning."

"Anything I should know about?"

"We'll get into it later." His expression remained inscrutable, but he shifted uncomfortably.

Thora recognized the body language. He wasn't as sure of himself as he wanted her to believe. Funny how after all these years she could still read him. At least, she liked to think so.

She strove for a conversational tone. "Claire means well, but she can sometimes be a pill."

"If by pill, you mean stubborn and opinionated, yeah. She isn't afraid to tell you how to get the job done if she thinks you're slacking."

"That's Claire. Some things don't change."

"Don't underestimate her," Will said. "She's a good one to have on your side."

"I know."

He ran a hand through his hair as he watched her from the foot of the bed. He looked tired. According to Claire, his day had started early that morning with her mother's frantic phone call. Despite exhaustion, he flashed one of those devastating smiles Thora remembered so well. "So, how are you really feeling?"

"I'm fine."

He cocked his head as he gazed down at her. "It's just us now. You can tell me the truth."

"You're starting to sound like Claire."

"I've been accused of worse. Let's try this again. How are you really feeling?"

She sighed. "If you must know, I seem to have a problem being alone but it's not something I want to talk about."

"Why not?"

She turned her head to the window. "No one wants to know how you're really doing. They say they do. They probably even think they do, but most people actually prefer platitudes. The truth makes them uncomfortable."

"You don't really believe that."

Her gaze cut back to him. "It's been my experience."

"Maybe you've been hanging out with the wrong people. Or maybe you're reading the room wrong."

She thought about her sister's insistence that Thora share her experience with the family rather than sweeping her emotions under the rug. She knew Claire loved her and wanted only the best for her, but the moment she revealed even a fraction of what she'd gone through these past few years, Claire would be the first to shut down. Despite her constant needling about openness and sharing, deep down she wanted to believe that her sister was still the tough, resilient warrior from their childhood. For the longest time now, Thora had felt she was anything but.

Will was still staring down at her. "You okay? I seemed to have hit a nerve."

She sighed. "Do you *really* want the truth?"

"No platitudes. Give it to me straight."

"A little while ago, I was lying here looking out the window and I started to shake. I couldn't stop. My chest tightened so painfully I thought for a moment I might be having a heart attack. Or that I'd wake up and find myself back in the box and my rescue was just a dream. That you were just a dream." She paused on a shiver. "How's that for candor?"

"Refreshing. And look. I'm still here."

Strange how easily it had all tumbled out when she'd spent years bottling everything up inside. Maybe those moments alone in the woods had broken the ice and lowered her natural reticence. Maybe deep down she still considered Will Dresden the best friend she'd never been able to replace. Whatever the reason, the past thirteen years suddenly seemed like the blink of an eye.

She lifted her hand to observe the tremors. "I'm still shaking."

"Of course you are. The combination of adrenaline, shock and fear can make for a powerful cocktail. Mix that with the residuals from whatever drug you were given, and I'd be amazed if you didn't have the shakes."

His pragmatic tone somehow made her feel better. "How long before it wears off?"

"The drug or the adrenaline? Everyone's different. Could take hours, days or even weeks before you feel back to normal. You need to give yourself time to heal no matter how long it takes."

She mustered a smile. "I'll take that under advisement, Dr. Dresden."

His gaze was steady and observant. She'd forgotten how intensely blue his eyes could be even in the most casual moments.

"What?"

He shrugged. "I was just thinking that in spite of the circumstances, it's good to see you."

Her heart jumped unexpectedly. "You, too."

"Wild reunion, huh?"

"As you said, one for the books."

He shook his head in awe. "Of all the ways I imagined we'd run into one another when I heard you were back, I never could have predicted this."

She fiddled with her ID bracelet. "How did you imagine we'd meet?"

"I don't know. One of the usual ways, I guess. The grocery store, the gas pumps. Maybe a restaurant. You've been back…what? Six months? Belfort hasn't grown that much. I was surprised when we never bumped into one another."

Was that disappointment she heard in his voice or wishful thinking in hers? "You could have just called me."

He propped his forearms on the footboard. "I thought about it. A lot, actually. But I didn't want to put you on the spot. You've been gone for a long time. We're not the same people we were when you left."

"You wouldn't have put me on the spot. I would have enjoyed hearing from you."

"Then why didn't you call me?"

An edge of something she couldn't define crept into his voice. "I wasn't sure you'd want to hear from me. I'm the one who left town." *Left you.*

"It wasn't all on you. I drove you to the airport. I could have asked you to stay before you got on that plane. I didn't."

"I used to wonder why."

"You knew why." He came around the side of the bed and perched on the edge as if the last thirteen years was like the blink of an eye for him, too. "Getting accepted into the FBI Academy was the chance of a lifetime. It was your dream."

"The dream was that we'd go to Quantico together."

"My circumstances changed so my dream had to change. But I wasn't about to hold you back. If I'd ask you to stay, you would have ended up resenting me for the rest of our lives."

"You don't know that."

"Yes, I do. We both do. And anyway, I like to think things have a way of working out the way they're supposed to."

She clasped her hands on top of the covers.

"I wish I believed that. In my experience, things sometimes go to hell no matter what you do."

His smile seemed sad and tender at the same time. "You've gotten cynical."

"I was just buried alive. I'd say I'm entitled."

"When you put it that way…"

He placed his hand against her cheek and for a split second they both froze, gazes locked. And then he leaned down and brushed his lips against her. It was barely a kiss. More comforting than sexual. She knew better than to read too much into it, and yet her pulse thudded in a way she hadn't experienced in a very long time.

Chapter Twelve

He drew away almost at once. "Sorry. I didn't mean—"

"No, don't be sorry." She looked pale and flawless in the hospital lighting. "It was nice. Comforting."

Might as well be talking about an old pair of shoes. Will felt sufficiently humbled as he stood and moved back to the end of the bed. "It's been… nice catching up, but we've got a lot to go over, so we should probably get started."

Her gaze followed him. Had her eyes always been that dark and soulful? That knowing?

She nodded. "Okay."

"We've had some new developments in the investigation. Things have happened that you should know about it."

She propped herself up against the pillows. "Things regarding my abduction?"

"Could be connected. We just aren't sure how."

"Well, that sounds intriguing. And infuriatingly vague. What's going on, Will?"

He took a moment to get his thoughts in order. Her eyes were a powerful distraction. They brought back a few too many explicit memories. "After you left in the ambulance, I did some exploring on my own. I located the old house we spoke about earlier. The one I photographed when we were kids."

She nodded. "The haunted house."

"You're teasing with that description, but you may not be as far off the mark as you might think."

Her amusement faded. "What do you mean?"

"I went searching for the house because I figured if the kidnappers knew about the cemetery, they'd also know about the homestead. And if they'd been inside, they might have left evidence."

She asked anxiously, "You found something?"

"More than I bargained for. I found another wooden container in an old shed behind the house. An air tube had already been affixed to the lid."

"What?" She bolted upright. *"Who—"*

"It was empty unless you count the poor rat that somehow got trapped."

"They must have been planning a second kidnapping," she said. "Do you know the identity of the intended victim?"

"If we assume the boxes are made to size, I'd say someone approximately my height and weight."

"You don't think—"

"No. I don't see them coming after me. I think

they'd rather have me running in circles looking for them."

"I hope you're right." She lay back against the pillows. "What about tire tracks, fingerprints, hair and fiber evidence?"

"We're still checking. I'll let you know if anything turns up."

She nodded, her fingers idly pleating the edge of the sheet. "Why do I get the feeling there's more to your discovery? What aren't you telling me, Will?"

"You always were perceptive." His smile was strained. "I noticed that some of the nails in a portion of the floor looked new. Like someone had recently hammered the planks back down. When I pried them up, I discovered skeletal remains beneath the shed. Human remains."

She looked so taken aback, he wondered if the news should have waited until morning. By her own admission, she was still suffering aftershocks from her kidnapping and burial, and likely would for some time to come. Will's instinct was to shield her from the disturbing discovery, but she was every bit the professional he was. Her experience and training had given her skills and the kind of insight that might be just what his team needed to fit the puzzle pieces together. Still, he needed to tread carefully. Since the moment he'd set foot in that shed, a dark premonition had hovered over him. He had a bad feeling that both he and Thora were being led down a path that neither had any wish to traverse.

"Have you identified the remains?"

He marveled at how normal her voice sounded after the shock of his disclosure. "We'll have to wait for the DNA analysis to know for sure."

"But you have some idea who the victim was?"

"We have clues," he said. "For one thing, the skull is small."

"A child?"

They exchanged solemn glances.

"We think the remains may be that of a missing boy named Danny Hagan. He disappeared ten years ago while walking home from school."

"Wait a minute," Thora said with a frown. "I know about that case."

"I'm sure you do. A missing child from your hometown would have gotten your attention."

She was already shaking her head. "That's not it. Last night at the pub, Logan Neville told me he and some of his students were working on a cold case that the local police had botched. He didn't mention the victim's name, only that the boy had vanished on his way home from school. Professor Neville has an incomplete police file, which he said he obtained by submitting a public information request. But he seems to think he can get access to the sealed records connected to the case through a confidential source at the police department."

"What source?"

"He didn't say."

Will's mind went back to that morning when he'd seen Neville leaving Elise Barrett's house. He wondered again what the two of them had been arguing about on her front porch. "Why did he tell you about the case?"

"He wanted to know if I'd take a look at the file. When I told him I'd think about it, he said I shouldn't wait too long. The boy's family deserves justice and the lead investigator needs to be held accountable. Will…he said you were the lead detective on that case." She took note of his expression and said, "He lied?"

"He got one thing right. The boy's family deserves justice."

"Why would he lie about something that could so easily be checked?"

"Seems to be a rash of that lately," Will muttered. "Maybe he thought attaching my name to the case would pique your interest. Or maybe accusing the new deputy chief of malfeasance and/ or incompetence makes for a more sensational podcast than putting the blame on a retired police detective."

"He does seem to crave attention and adoration," Thora said. "But I still don't understand what any of this has to do with my abduction."

"Maybe nothing. Maybe everything."

"That's not an answer." When he didn't immediately respond, she said, "You're still holding back. Don't do that."

He walked over to the window and glanced out. The moon was up, a shimmering sliver hanging just above the skyline. It reminded him of the tree-house and the countless nights they'd spent gazing up at the stars. He suddenly longed for the innocence of those hot summer evenings.

"Will?"

He shook off the memories and turned. "I need to ask a tough question. I think I know the answer, but I have to be certain. Have you been to see James Ellis Ridgeway in the past few weeks?"

She gaped at him in astonishment. "Why on earth would you ask that?"

"Can you please just answer me?"

"I've *never* been to see Ridgeway. I've never spoken to him or corresponded with him in any way. What does he have to do with my kidnapping? Or with that child's remains?"

"That's what we're trying to determine," Will said. "Correct me if I'm wrong, but some of his earliest victims were kids."

"Five that we know of before he graduated to adult females. We think he considered the children practice before he refined his MO and moved on to his real targets."

"Do you remember the locations of those bodies?"

"They were dumped or buried in rural locations a few miles outside of metropolitan areas." She recited them without the slightest hesitation. "Mobile, Alabama; Gulfport, Mississippi; Baton Rouge, Louisiana; El Paso, Texas; and Las Cruces, New Mexico."

"All up and down I-10," he said. "Belfort isn't exactly in the middle, but it's certainly along his route."

"Will." She said nothing else for a moment. Then in a hushed voice, "Do you realize the implication? The discovery of a sixth child victim could mean there are more we haven't found yet. That we don't even know about."

"Is it so surprising? Ridgeway admitted to withholding the locations and identities of some of his victims for leverage. We have no idea how many could still be out there."

She grew pensive. Whatever emotions she might be feeling were well hidden behind her professional facade. "Last night before Professor Neville told me about the case, he asked if I would be willing to be a guest on his podcast. He wanted to interview me along with a freelance reporter who's writing a book about the Weatherman. Professor Neville said the reporter had been to see Ridgeway in prison and that my name had been mentioned."

Will nodded. "We know about the reporter. His name is Noah Asher. Earlier today, I found him inside your townhouse."

Her eyes widened. "How did he get in? And what was he doing in my home?"

"He claimed the back door was open. He said he was looking for evidence that had been overlooked when your townhouse was processed by CSU."

"What kind of evidence?"

"According to Asher, something that would prove the Weatherman was behind your abduction."

Her mask dropped for a moment, giving him a glimpse of her raw emotions. Dread, outrage. More than a touch of fear. "Did he find anything?"

"Not that we know of. But we've since learned that he's been going to see Ridgeway every month for the past two years. Their connection is apparently a lot stronger than he let on. We know he was in the pub last night before your abduction."

"The guy at the bar."

Will nodded. "We took him into custody on a misdemeanor, questioned him and then had to cut him loose. We'll keep him under surveillance for as long as our manpower and resources hold out. Or until he leaves town." Will paused. "Are you okay? I'm throwing a lot at you at once and this business with Ridgeway is bound to be unsettling."

"It's a lot to take in," she agreed. "But I'm glad you're being honest with me. I'd rather know than not know."

"That's what I figured."

"There's something you should probably know," she told him. "Professor Neville was the second person to bring up the Weatherman to me last night."

"Who was the first?"

"Elise Barrett. Do you know her?" She searched his face. "Of course you do. She said she'd been with the Belfort PD since college."

"I know her," Will said without inflection. "What did she say about Ridgeway?"

"That she'd always been fascinated by the case and wondered if their paths might have crossed during a killing spree that took him through Belfort."

"That's a strange thing to wonder about." Particularly since he'd never once heard her mention James Ellis Ridgeway when they were together.

Thora shrugged. "People are fascinated by serial killers. She also asked if I'd ever considered the possibility that Ridgeway could have been responsible for Michael's death."

"She said that to you?" His irritation at Elise took the sting out of hearing Thora mention her husband's name for the first time. Will was glad she could bring her marriage into the conversation so openly. He wouldn't want her to feel the need to hide that part of her life. He couldn't say with complete honesty that he was happy she'd found love, but he was deeply sorry she'd lost it.

"It's not like I haven't wondered the same thing," she admitted. "Michael died in a traffic accident. Someone ran a red light and broadsided his vehicle. There was no evidence linking Ridgeway to the crash, and he never claimed credit..." She trailed off. "But I still wondered."

"You were looking for answers," Will said. "It's human nature to try and make sense of a tragedy."

"Even when there are no answers."

"Even then." When his dad died, Thora had been the only one who'd been able to offer even a vestige of comfort and understanding. He wished that he could have been there for her during the worst time of her life, but that wouldn't have been appropriate or even welcome.

"Do you think it could be true?" she asked in a hushed voice.

"That Ridgeway was involved? I guess it's possible, but not very likely," Will said. "Even if it were true, it wouldn't be your fault."

"I know." But she looked haunted by the possibility.

He wondered if it was a good idea to keep going. Everything that had happened in past twenty-four hours had taken a heavy emotional toll. "Maybe I should clear out and let you get some sleep."

"But we're not finished yet, are we?"

"The rest can wait."

"No, don't go. I'm fine. We need to get through this and besides..."

She didn't want to be alone. Will could still read her, too. "Let's go back to the conversation with Elise for a moment. In the interest of full disclosure, you should know that we used to go out."

"You and Elise? That explains some things," she murmured, then glanced up. "Was it serious?"

"It was until it wasn't. I only bring it up because your sister told me this morning that Elise still has a chip on her shoulder from our breakup. At Claire's request, I went to see her."

"You think she might be involved?"

"Not really, but I needed to have a conversation with her to set my mind at ease. It didn't. She made it clear I'm not her favorite person these days. She blames me for getting her transferred from Criminal Investigations to Internal Affairs after we split up."

"Did you?"

"No. She was a good detective. I wouldn't do that."

Thora seemed to ponder the new information. "As much as I appreciate your candor, I still don't understand what any of this has to do with Ridgeway."

"I'm still getting to that." He moved back to her bedside as he scrolled through his texts. Then he sat down on the edge and handed her the phone. "This is an entry from the visitors' log at the Donaldson Correctional Facility from almost two weeks ago."

She took the phone, scanned the image and then her gaze shot back to his. "That's not my handwriting, although it does look similar. Someone obviously took the time to practice my signature, but I've never been to that prison."

"I believe you. Someone either faked your ID or stole the real one to gain access to Ridgeway. Where do you keep your personal belongings when you're in class?"

"Locked in my office. Bottom desk drawer."

"Your driver's license never went missing?"

"If it did, it couldn't have been gone for long. I would have noticed."

"What about your passport?"

"I keep it in a drawer in my bedroom." She looked taken aback as if something had suddenly occurred to her. "Will, my ID wasn't the only thing taken."

"What do you mean?" Instead of getting up and putting distance between them like he should have, he remained perched on the edge of her bed. She didn't appear to mind or even to notice. Her brow was furrowed in deep concentration.

"I had a medallion on a silver chain in my hand earlier when I was brought into the ER. They bagged it up with my clothes and other personal effects. Someone dropped that medallion down the air tube early this morning."

"Why didn't you tell me before now?" Will asked.

"I don't know. Maybe I wasn't thinking clearly. I was in a daze when you pulled me out of that box. The next thing I knew, I was in an ambulance, then the ER…this is the first chance I've had to really talk to you. To think about what happened. I kept that medallion in a jewelry box in the same drawer as my passport. Someone must have found it when they were looking for my ID."

"If they went to the trouble of dropping it down the air tube, it must have some significance to you."

"It belonged to Michael." Her gaze met his as her fingers slid across the bed covers. For a moment, he thought she meant to take his hand, but instead she smoothed an invisible wrinkle from the blanket. "It was a gift from his grandfather. He never took it off. He had it on the day he died."

"I'm sorry."

Her hand lifted from the blanket as if to let him know she was okay. "Somehow, Ridgeway figured out it belonged to Michael, and he knew that it would have an emotional impact on me, especially while I was trapped in the box."

"Let's not get ahead of ourselves," Will cautioned. "Ridgeway's involvement is only a theory at this point."

"I lived with him in my head for so long, it's hard not to let my imagination get the better of me," she admitted. "You mentioned videos earlier. I'd like to see them."

"Do you really think that's a good idea?"

"Analyzing information is what I've been doing for the past decade. Maybe I can help."

Wordlessly, he queued up the first video and handed her his phone. Then he watched her as she watched the grainy footage. The only sound in the room was the beating of her fists against the container lid and her plaintive query, "Can anyone hear me? What do you want? Just tell me what you want!"

She glanced up once, met his gaze and then kept her eyes glued to the video. She played it again all the way through before she moved on to the second video, which she also repeated.

"It really was like looking for a needle in a haystack," she murmured.

"As I said earlier, we had some help. I could point out the markers, but they don't look like much without enlarging the individual frames. You should also take a look at the text messages below the videos."

She scrolled through the texts, then read them a second and third time aloud using different inflections.

"What do you think?" Will finally asked.

"They're interesting on a couple of levels," she said. "Other than the mention of my name, the thing that stands out is the tone. Texting is a very casual form of communication. We tend to text the same way we speak except in an abbreviated format. These messages have an unusual formality. It makes me wonder if the tone is real or if the sender is trying to disguise his or her true voice." Her eyes remained glued to the screen. "Does the literary reference mean anything to you?"

"I know the Moriarty character is a villain in some of the Sherlock Holmes stories, but the reference doesn't mean anything to me personally."

"He's more than a villain, especially in recent adaptations. He's an archenemy, a nemesis. A cold, brilliant mastermind who considers himself the detective's equal or better. He uses his intellect and cunning to devise cruel and sometimes personal ways to best Sherlock Holmes. Whoever kidnapped and buried me alive is also cruel and cunning. And they made it personal. For whatever reason, they feel the need to prove their superior skill and intellect. I'm guessing that's why you don't think the second box is meant for you."

"Like I said, you've always been perceptive."

She glanced up. "They don't want to kill you. They want to destroy you."

THORA COULD HEAR someone on the other end of the air tube. The drumming was faint. Tap, tap… pause…tap, tap. The sound kept repeating until she came awake on a gasp, instinctively lifting her hands to press against the lid of the container. Her palms met nothing but air. It was dark, but not as dark as the box.

Still, her heart pounded in terror as she glanced around, frantic to remember where she was. Slowly, shapes formed in the darkness as everything came back to her. She was in the hospital still hooked up to an IV drip. But she wasn't alone.

From her periphery, she saw a shadow rise from the darkness. *It's okay. It's just Mom or Claire.* Her mother had insisted on spending the night, but Claire had made her leave at some point, promising to stay and keep an eye on Thora even though a guard was stationed outside her room.

You're safe. No one can get to you in here.

Not her kidnappers. Not the Weatherman.

But her heart continued to hammer, and she tried to scramble away as the shadow moved toward her.

"Thora? Hey, it's Will. Can you hear me? You're okay. You're safe." He moved closer to the bed so that she could see his face in the moonlight streaming in through the window.

"Will?" His name came out as a tremulous whisper. "You came back?"

"Yes, a few hours ago. I'm sorry if I startled you."

"I wasn't expecting you. I thought—"

"What's wrong?" His voice sounded both gentle and mysterious in the dark.

"I thought I heard tapping."

"Tapping?"

"Like this." She drummed the sequence on the

mattress. "They wouldn't give me water until I responded with the same repetition. At least, that's the way it seemed."

"Sounds like a control thing," he said. "They wanted to make you submit."

"And I did," she said. "For another drink of water."

"You did what you had to do to stay alive. That's a good thing."

She shivered. "Are you sure you didn't hear anything just now?"

"Just hospital noises in the hallway."

She tried to relax but her teeth chattered from nerves and the frigid AC. "I guess it was just a bad dream."

"You're bound to have them after what you've been through."

"You said it would take time." As the fog lifted, she lay back against the pillows and drew in cleansing breaths until her heart calmed and her pulse evened.

"Do you want me to turn on a light?"

"No, it's okay. I can see you." She glanced past him into the room. "Where's Claire?"

"She was exhausted. I promised I wouldn't leave your side if she'd go home and get some rest."

"I'm surprised you were able to talk her into it."

He smiled down at her. "I can be persuasive when I need to be."

"I remember. I'm glad she went home, but you don't have to stay. I'm okay." Of course, she wasn't okay and they both knew it. Her time in the box would haunt her for a very long time, possibly for the rest of her life. Even now, wide awake and in Will's company, a tiny part of her wondered if this was a dream. If she was still lying in that buried box with nothing but the mirage of Will Dresden to keep her from losing hope.

"Tell me about your dream," he said.

"There isn't much more to tell. I just remember the drumming or tapping. The sequence kept repeating in my head. Over and over and over. Like that sound has been ingrained in my subconscious."

"It'll fade in time." He was still at her bedside, peering down at her in the dark. "Are you sure you're okay? Can I get you anything?"

"Why is it so cold in here? I can't seem to stop shivering."

"Hospital rooms are always cold." He tucked the covers around her shoulders. "Better?"

"Some."

"Hold on, I'll see if I can scrounge up an extra blanket."

"No, don't go!" She hadn't meant to sound so adamant. "Sorry."

"Your teeth are chattering."

"I'll be okay in a minute."

He hesitated, then said, "Move over."

"Will—"

"You're freezing and I have body heat to spare. That's all this is."

She scooted to the side and he lay down, spooning her body against his. "How's that?"

"Better." His warmth was dangerously addictive. "Will?"

"Yeah?"

"Why are you doing this?"

"It's not a big deal. I'm just trying to warm you up."

"I don't mean this." She tugged his arm around her. "Why are you here at all? You said it yourself. We're not the same people we were thirteen years ago."

"So? I can't show you a little kindness? I can't still care about you?" His breath fanned against her hair. "You could have stayed gone for another thirteen years and a part of me would still care about you. A part of me would still miss you every single day."

She closed her eyes. "I missed you, too."

It was very quiet in the room. Even the routine hospital noises from the hallway had faded. She and Will might have had the whole floor to themselves. The darkness cocooned them, protected them. But even as she relaxed in the safety of his arms, her internal clock reminded her that twenty-four hours ago she was just waking up in the box.

As if sensing her distress, he said in a calming voice, "I saw the tree house today."

"At Mom's house? Hard to believe it's still there after so many years."

"Built to last even through hurricanes," he said. "Seeing it this morning brought back a lot of memories. Remember the neighborhood water balloon wars?"

"How could I forget? You and I made a good team."

"Deadly, some might say."

She found herself smiling in the dark. "I loved that tree house. I loved lying out there after dark and staring up at the stars." She said in the softest voice, "My first time was in that tree house."

"I know. So was mine." His baritone was a low rumble against her ear.

She rolled to her back and stared up at the ceiling. "We were both pretty naive. I seem to recall a lot of fumbling."

"And yet..."

"It was magical," she said on a dreamy sigh.

"And only got better with practice. A lot of practice, as I recall."

She turned her head to face him. "We probably shouldn't be having this conversation."

His amusement faded. "Because of Michael?"

"Because it makes the past thirteen years seem as if they never happened. But they did. We've both been through a lot since I left Belfort."

"I know. I'm sorry."

"I'm not just talking about my husband's death. I haven't told anyone the real reason I moved back home."

He rolled to his back so their heads were lying side by side on the pillows, as if they were once again gazing up at the stars. "You can tell me."

"Remember earlier when I said people don't really want to know how you're doing? I've had some experience with that kind of social awkwardness."

"What happened?"

"I had a panic attack at work. I've experienced a few over the years, but this was a bad one. A coworker found me huddled in the corner of my cubicle. I couldn't walk, I couldn't speak. I barely even knew where I was. It was as terrifying as waking up in the box. Maybe more so. I spent some time in the hospital."

"I didn't know."

"No one did. I kept it from my mom because she's always been such a worrier and she's had a few health scares of her own lately. Which is another reason I moved back. Anyway, in order to return to work, I had to be cleared by a therapist. She helped me learn how to deal with my repressed grief and guilt, and she taught me ways to cope with the darker aspects of my job. Eventually, things returned to normal, but the episode had to be noted in my file. It shouldn't have mattered, but I knew that it would."

"So you left the FBI and came home."

"Yes. I wanted to be near my family."

He said without a hint of awkwardness, "I'm glad you told me."

"I felt you should know."

He turned his head to stare at her. "Why?"

"Because it's not too late to walk away."

"I don't walk away," he said. "I learned the hard way not to give up without a fight."

Chapter Thirteen

Will left the hospital early Sunday morning and went home to shower and change clothes. Pulling on a pair of jeans, he lay down on the bed for a few minutes to think. He hadn't slept much in the past twenty-four hours and the rotation of the ceiling fan blades made him drowsy and lethargic. He only meant to close his eyes for a moment, but the next thing he knew, his phone woke him up. He glanced at the time. After nine. He'd planned to leave early enough to drop by the hospital to see Thora before her release, but now he was already running late for a meeting at the station with Reyes.

He answered his phone and put Reyes on speaker as he finished getting dressed.

"I went by Logan Neville's house again this morning," the detective told him. "No one answered the door and his car wasn't in the driveway. Maybe he left town for the weekend."

"You tried his phone?"

"Went straight to voice mail."

"Are you already at the station?"

"Just waiting on you, boss."

"Okay, give me a few minutes," Will said. "I'll swing by the U-SET campus on my way in."

"You think he'll be in the office on a Sunday morning?"

"He has to be somewhere," Will said. "Keep me posted if you hear from him."

Ten minutes later, Will found a parking place near the Criminology Department, an ugly brick-and-glass building that spoiled an otherwise attractive campus. In his final two years of college, he'd spent most of his time in that building. Back then, he could have found his way around the classrooms and hallways with his eyes closed, but that was before recent renovations had significantly changed the layout. A custodian let him in through the main entrance when he flashed his badge.

"Can you point me in the direction of Professor Neville's office?"

"Sixth floor, straight down the hallway, last door on the left. I doubt he's in, though. Classes ended on Friday. Most everyone's already cleared out."

"What about Professor Graham's office?"

"Same floor, first door off the elevator."

Will thanked him before heading for the elevators. The building seemed unnaturally quiet, as empty classrooms and lecture halls tended to be.

Except for the custodian, he didn't see anyone around. The car bumped to a stop and the doors slid open. He stepped out and stood for a moment staring down the long hallway before he located Thora's office and tried the door. To his surprise, the knob turned and the door opened without a sound. Odd, because he would have thought she'd locked up before leaving on Friday.

Sunlight streamed into the small room from a long window directly across from the door. A leather chair faced the desk and behind the workspace, a credenza accommodated stacks of papers, file folders and books. Like her townhouse, the office lacked any personal touches. Even the crowded bookcases seemed impersonal with dozens of psychology and criminology volumes that could have belonged to anyone. The featureless space reminded Will that for all he knew, Thora's time in Belfort was transitory.

Snapping on a pair of gloves, he sat down behind the desk and tried the bottom drawer where she kept her personal belongings. He didn't know what he expected to find. She would have taken her purse and wallet with her when she left on Friday. The only thing that remained was an umbrella, a small makeup bag and a first aid kit.

He removed and examined each item. As he placed them back in the drawer one by one, he noticed a single hair had been caught in the zipper of the makeup bag. Not the brunette strand that he would have expected to find among Thora's belongings, but an auburn spiral that made him think instantly of Elise Barrett.

Carefully, he untangled the strand from the zipper and placed it in a small evidence bag. Then he returned everything to the drawer and was getting ready to leave when the ping of the elevator drew him out into the hallway. Someone had just stepped inside. He tried to catch a glimpse of the passenger, but the doors slid closed too quickly. For some reason, he felt a strong compulsion to find out who was on the elevator. He located the stairwell and took the steps two at a time down to the ground level. The elevator didn't stop but continued to the basement. Probably the custodian, he decided.

He got in the second elevator and went back up to the sixth floor, then followed the directions to Logan Neville's office. His door was also ajar but unlike Thora's office, the space was occupied. A young woman dressed in jeans and a navy T-shirt reclined in a swivel chair, her bare feet propped up on the desk. She had a sheath of papers in her left hand and a red marker in her right.

He checked the name on the door and knocked.

"Go away. I'm busy," she said in a bored drawl.

He pushed open the door. "Sorry for the interruption. I'm looking for Logan Neville."

"Obviously, he's not here," she said without looking up.

Will glanced down the hallway toward the elevators. "I didn't just miss him, did I?"

"Not unless you know something I don't," she muttered.

"Do you know where I can find him?"

"Who's asking?"

"Deputy Chief Will Dresden."

That got her attention. She laid the papers and marker aside and swung her legs off the desk. She looked to be in her early twenties, suntanned and fit, with thick blond hair and light blue eyes rimmed with lashes so long they had to be fake. She wore no other makeup except for a shiny glaze on her lips.

"This is quite the coincidence," she said in that same detached drawl. "By all means, come in." She waved him toward the chair across from the desk.

He hesitated for a split second before he moved into the office and took a seat. "Why is it a coincidence?"

"Professor Neville recently conducted an hourlong lecture on you."

"On me? That's a pretty dry subject," Will said.

"To the contrary, he's always been concerned about nepotism and legacy hires in mid-to large-size police departments." She gave him a long scrutiny. "I do most of his research. After digging into your background so thoroughly, I find it a little strange seeing you in person like this."

"Thoroughly, huh? And here I don't even know your name," he said.

"Addison March. I'm Professor Neville's TA." Her gaze was very direct, as if she knew the impact of her attractiveness and dared him to react to it.

He didn't. He returned her stare with nothing more than casual curiosity. "You may be just the person who can tell me how to reach him."

A frown flickered. "Have you tried him at home?"

"He's not answering his door or his phone."

"Well, then, he's probably already gone."

"Where?" Will asked.

She shrugged. "His usual summer sabbatical. He never tells anyone his destination. Even me."

"When was the last time you saw him?"

"We were together at Molly's Pub on Friday night. We meet there almost every weekend unless something more important comes up."

"By we, do you mean you and Professor Neville or you, Professor Neville and the rest of his team?"

She twisted her blond hair into a rope and draped it over one shoulder. "How do you know about our team?"

"Word gets around. It's not a secret, is it?"

"Hardly, but we try to be discreet. It's been our experience that the CID detectives can be particularly territorial if they feel threatened. They don't like to be shown up, especially by students, but I imagine you would know better than me about egos and insecurities." She cocked her head as she gazed at him across the desk. "I do have to wonder who you've been talking to, though. Let me take a wild guess. Baylee Fisher came to see you, didn't she?"

Will kept his expression and tone neutral. "Is she a friend of yours?"

Addison dismissed the notion with a roll of her eyes. "Please. Baylee is far too jealous and emotionally immature to have friends. She can be clever and occasionally useful, but she and I are most definitely not friends."

"Then how did you know she came to see me?"

"It wasn't hard to deduce. When we heard what happened to Professor Graham, Baylee claimed to have information that could help the police find her."

"What information?"

"She wouldn't say. That's a big part of her problem. She's not a team player. And she's prone to exaggeration."

"What if I told you she came to see me before she knew about the abduction?"

Addison smiled. "Then I would remind you of what I said at the beginning of this conversation. She's a very clever girl. Maybe that's what she wanted you to think. But you didn't come here to talk about Baylee Fisher, did you?"

"No, I didn't. Have you spoken to Professor Neville since Friday night?"

"Nope. When he's gone, he's gone." She folded her arms on the desk and leaned forward. "What's all this about, anyway? Why are you so interested in Logan... Dr. Neville's whereabouts?"

"I just need to ask him a few questions," Will said.

The long lashes blinked slowly. "Why don't you ask me instead? Maybe I can help you."

"Okay. For starters, I'd like to talk about the cold case that seems to have caught your team's interest."

"You meaning the missing boy? What about it?"

"Professor Neville told a colleague that a confidential source in the police department could provide access to sealed records connected to that case. I'd like to know who his source is."

She looked disappointed. "You came all the way over here to ask about case files?"

"Sealed records are exempt from public information requests. They can only be accessed by law enforcement personnel or by court order," he told her. "We take security breaches very seriously, particularly when the leak can compromise an investigation."

"What investigation? That case had languished in the archives for nearly a decade until it came to our attention." When he failed to offer a counterargument, she leaned back in the chair with a pensive frown. "Can we speak hypothetically?"

"Sure."

She got up to close the door and then came around to perch on the edge of the desk. "What if I told you there's a certain cop who has an ax to grind for the way she's been treated by your department? What if I told you that Professor Neville has a way of finding a person's weakness and using it to get what he wants? He's an expert at drawing people in who can be useful to him. When he's done..." She dusted off her hands. "He's done."

"That doesn't paint a very flattering picture of the man," Will said. "You aren't afraid he'll do the same to you?"

She smiled. "My eyes are wide open when it comes to Logan Neville. I'm a complete realist. I know how to get what I want, too."

"I don't doubt it, but we seem to be getting a little off track."

"No, we're not. It's all connected." She crossed her legs and leaned back on one arm. "Let's say the person who accessed those sealed files was the aggrieved cop. Say she's the one who brought the case to Professor Neville in the first place. She has something to prove and she thought *he* could be useful to *her*." She gave Will a curious smile. "Do you follow so far?"

"Trying to."

"The cop had begun an investigation on her own but soon became desperate for a fresh pair of eyes. She couldn't ask anyone in the police department for help, so she came to Professor Neville. All he had to do was convince her that getting access to those sealed records was paramount to cracking the case. Once he had what he wanted, he'd no longer need said cop." She straightened. "Now do you get the picture?"

"Why would he shut her out of the investigation once he had the records?"

"Because solving this case could be big. Mind-blowing big. Like book-deal big for someone with the right contacts. Why share the limelight when you can claim all the glory for yourself?"

"What makes this case so big?" Will asked.

"If I told you that, you might decide you want the glory."

"Does it have anything to do with James Ellis Ridgeway?"

Her eyes widened. "Who told you that?"

"I think you just did."

Her mask dropped back into place. "Why would you think the Weatherman had anything to do with a nine-year-old boy's disappearance? He preyed on women."

"Not in the beginning," Will said. "Is that why Professor Neville invited Noah Asher to be a guest on his podcast? Asher has a relationship with Ridgeway. He could provide the professor access to the Weatherman. But I'm not telling you anything you don't already know, am I? Does he plan to drop Asher, too, when he gets what he wants?"

All of a sudden, Addison didn't look bored or amused. "You may be smarter than she gives you credit for."

"Who?"

"Again, hypothetically, I'd recommend you take a look at a certain redhead in Internal Affairs who seems prone to obsessions and grudges. She used to hang out with us at the pub and offer unsolicited advice until she and Professor Neville had a falling out."

"Over the case?"

Her smile turned smug. "Among other things."

Will remembered Baylee's claim that Addison March and Logan Neville were sleeping together, which was why, according to Baylee, the TA got all the plum assignments. Ordinarily, he might be concerned for a young woman who had fallen under the spell of a man like Logan Neville, but he had a feeling the professor had met his match.

"Your promotion really sent her over the edge," Addison said. "She claimed when the two of you were partners, she did all the real police work while you coasted by on your looks and legacy."

"Just to be clear, are we talking about Elise Barrett?"

"I'd rather not mention names." Addison

hopped off the desk and went back around to plop down in the chair. She swiveled for a moment, her gaze steady and mocking. "You know why she started working that particular case? She thought if she could prove her investigative skills were superior to yours, she'd be reinstated as a detective in CID. And she'd take you down a peg in the process. This won't come as a surprise, but the woman *really* doesn't like you, Deputy Chief."

"So it would seem." He rose and tossed his card on the desk. "If you hear from Professor Neville, ask him to give me a call."

She didn't bother picking up the card. "Before you go, can I ask you a question?"

"Go ahead."

"It's about Professor Graham. Her kidnapping and rescue have been all over the local news. I don't know her personally, and to be honest, I was never that keen to have her on staff. I don't find her credentials all that impressive. She wasn't even a field agent. But no one deserves to go through what she did. Do you have any idea who could have done something like that to her?"

"We have leads, but I really can't say much more at this time."

She went on as if he hadn't answered. "To be trapped in a box like that and then once freed, to realize that the monster who kidnapped and buried you alive could be someone you know, someone you work with, someone you see on a regular basis. Someone still plotting your demise. How would you ever get over something like that?"

"By finding and locking up the person or persons responsible," Will said.

"Do you think that will happen, though? What's the clearance rate for the Belfort Police Department? Thirty percent?"

"A little higher than the national average."

She gave him a disparaging look. "In other words, nothing to brag about. Which is why you have so many cold cases on your hands. Which is also why Professor Neville put our team together. We can help if you'll let us."

Will moved to the door. "Thanks for the offer. I'll keep it in mind."

"You won't because your ego will get in the way, but you should. We're very good at what we do." She rose, too. "With the right resources and contacts, we could probably find Professor Graham's kidnapper within the week."

"I admire your confidence."

"Why shouldn't we be confident? We have the skills and know-how to back it up. Not to mention youth and energy." She came around the desk to see him out. "I wonder if you'd be interested in a wager, Deputy Chief. A challenge, if you will. Our team against yours."

That stopped Will cold and he turned. "This isn't a game. You're talking about a woman's life."

"I'm well aware of the stakes."

"Are you?" Will's voice dropped. "Let's get one thing straight. If you or any of your teammates interfere in our investigation in any way, you'll be slapped with a sizeable fine and thrown in jail for at least ninety days. You won't like the accommodations, I promise you."

"We'll take that under advisement." She leaned a shoulder against the door and folded her arms. She was still watching him when he got to the end of the hallway.

AFTER WILL CONCLUDED his meeting at the station with Reyes, he drove over to Elise Barrett's place and parked at the curb. The scent of the neighbor's roses bombarded him as he got out of the car and started toward the house. Before he reached the porch steps, another vehicle pulled to the curb. Instinctively, he stepped off the walkway, using the dense foliage for cover as he watched and waited. He expected to see Elise or even Logan Neville coming his way. The sight of Thora took him completely by surprise.

She didn't see him until she was almost to the steps. Then she visibly started as her hand flew to her heart on a gasp.

"Will! You scared me half to death. What are you doing hiding in Elise Barrett's front yard?"

She glanced toward the porch. "This is her house, isn't it?"

"I wasn't exactly hiding and the better question is why are you here?"

"For the same reason as you, I imagine. I have questions." She cast another glance toward the house and lowered her voice. "Is she home?"

"I haven't knocked yet." He motioned for her to follow him back to the street where they would be out of earshot. "When did you get out of the hospital?"

"A little while ago. Claire drove me home and agreed to stay at the townhouse and wait for the locksmith." She tucked her hair behind her ears, highlighting the darkness of her eyes and the paleness of her skin. How was it possible, Will wondered, that she could come through such a nightmare and still look as appealing as the day he'd driven her to the airport thirteen years ago?

"I'm surprised she let you out of her sight," he said.

"I know. Much less borrow her car, but I can be stubborn, too, when I need to be." She glanced past Will up the walkway and her expression subtly altered. The haunted look he'd noticed the night before flitted across her features. "I keep thinking about my conversation with Elise at the pub. Why would the notion even occur to her that Ridgeway might be responsible for Michael's accident?"

"You said you'd wondered the same thing," Will reminded her.

"That's different. At the time of the accident, I'd been on the Weatherman case for more than two years. He and his victims had become a part of my daily work life. But Elise has no apparent connection to the case. Why would she care enough to even speculate? Unless she's the one who stole my ID and went to see Ridgeway in person. Maybe he said something to her about Michael's accident. Did he claim credit, plant a seed?" She let out a breath. "I have so many questions running through my head, Will. You can't imagine what I've been thinking or the rabbit holes I've fallen into. If Elise really has been in touch with Ridgeway, I need to know what he said to her."

"We'll find out," Will promised. "One way or another. But you have to let me handle this. I know Elise. If we both confront her, she'll feel cornered and either lash out or button up."

"Then let me talk to her alone."

His response was visceral and not very tactful. "That's a bad idea."

"Why? You said yourself you're not her favorite person at the moment. She still has a chip on her shoulder from the breakup. Maybe she'll talk to me."

He lowered his voice as he cast a quick glance toward the house. "Let's assume for a minute that she is the one who used your ID to visit Ridgeway. Have you taken the supposition a step further and wondered if she might have somehow been involved in your abduction? Do you think she'll admit to everything and go with you quietly to the police station? The Elise I know won't go down without a fight."

She touched his arm briefly. The gesture seemed almost protective and somehow deeply intimate. "This can't be easy for you. Do you really think she's involved?"

He took a moment to answer her. "I don't know. I have a hard time believing the woman I've known for years—much less the detective I worked with—is capable of something so brutally cruel, but, like you, I have questions."

"Then let's go hear what she has to say."

"Thora—"

She'd already turned and started up the walkway. Short of physically blocking her path, there was nothing he could do but follow her up the steps and across the porch to the entrance. The wooden door stood open, allowing the midday heat to invade the house through the screen.

"That's odd," she said. "I can hear the air conditioner running at the side of the house. Why would she leave the door open? Do you think she knows we're here?"

"One way to find out." Will reached around her and rapped on the door frame.

Thora cupped her hands and peered through the screen. "I can't see anything. It's too dim inside and too bright out here."

"Maybe we should give her time to get to the door before you go all Peeping Tom," he suggested.

"Will." She sounded tense. "Does this look like blood to you?"

He moved around her to examine the red smears where a bloody hand had clutched the edge of the screen door. Then he knelt and touched a finger to a droplet on the concrete floor. "It's fresh."

"Is that enough to constitute exigent circumstances?"

"I would say so. Besides, I've already conducted one warrantless search this weekend. Might as well go for two." He pounded on the door frame and called out Elise's name. "It's Will. Are you home?" He listened for a moment then stared through the screen just as Thora had done. "Elise, are you okay?"

"Can you see anything?" Thora asked.

"No sign of life."

She pulled a pair of latex gloves from her bag and snapped them on. At his look of amazement, she said, "I saw a box at the hospital and thought they might come in handy. I've got spares if you need them."

"Thanks, I've got my own."

She tried the screen door. It opened with a creak. "Shouldn't we go in and see if she's okay?"

"You wait out here," he said. "Circumstances have changed and I have a badge. Let me check things out before we both invade her privacy."

"Maybe you should glove up first in case we're dealing with a crime scene."

"Let's hope that's not the case." But blood at an open door was never a good sign.

"If I don't hear back from you in five minutes, I'm coming in," Thora warned.

Will called out Elise's name as he pulled open the screen door and stepped inside. Pausing to listen for signs of a struggle or distress, he moved cautiously from one room to the next. He found more blood drops on the bathroom floor and watery smears in the sink where someone had tried to clean up.

Backtracking into the kitchen, he went out the rear door to the shady patio where Elise spent most of her time. He checked the garage and behind the gate before going back inside to collect blood samples from the bathroom. Pocketing the evidence, he glanced inside the primary bedroom and then the room at the end of the hall that she used as a home office.

The space was just large enough to accommodate a desk and chair and a small sofa beneath the windows. On the opposite wall from the desk, she'd pinned copies of newspaper articles to a large old-school corkboard. Will went over to the desk and sorted through the stacks of folders. They contained police reports and interview transcripts from the Danny Hagan case. He remembered the hours he and Elise had logged going door to door, searching abandoned buildings, walking untold miles along creek banks, poking through underbrush and overflowing dumpsters. Eventually, they'd been assigned to other investigations and Danny Hagan had become another missing child statistic.

Newspaper clippings about the disappearance had been stuck to the corkboard, along with dozens of pieces chronicling the Weatherman's gruesome sprees. Next to the corkboard, she'd taped a map to the wall and pinned the locations of his kills along I-10. She'd obviously been trying to connect the missing boy to James Ellis Ridgeway. She used red pins to designate his known victims and a yellow pin to represent Danny's disappearance.

Will stood studying the map and the newspaper clippings until Thora called out to him from the porch.

"Will? Everything okay?"

"Hang on! I'll be right out."

He snapped a few shots of the corkboard and map before he went back over to the desk and tried the drawers. Most of them were filled with the usual office paraphernalia, but the bottom left drawer looked suspiciously shallow compared to the one on the right. He removed a stack of papers and knocked on the wood bottom. Then he slid his hand to the back of the drawer and felt for a notch. The false panel lifted up revealing an empty envelope with a Donaldson Correctional Facility return address.

"Will?"

"I'm coming." He replaced the false bottom and returned the contents to the drawer before going back out to the living room.

Thora stood in front of the built-in bookcases perusing the titles. She glanced over her shoulder when he came into the room. "You didn't find Elise?"

"No, but there's more blood in the bathroom."

"That can't be good. What should we do?"

"For one thing, you should go back outside," he said. "You're not supposed to be in here."

"I know, but when you didn't return, I got worried. I was afraid you might have run into trouble." She turned back to the bookcases. "Come take a look at this."

He moved across the room and stood beside her. "What are we looking at?"

"Middle of the top row. A collection of Sherlock Holmes stories."

"Not exactly a smoking gun," Will said. "You'd be surprised how many people give books like that as gifts to cops. They think we all like detective stories."

"Don't you?"

"I'm more of a history buff."

"Good to know."

They spun simultaneously toward the foyer as the screen door slammed closed. Elise came through the cased opening and stopped short when she saw them. Her bandaged hand went automatically to her shoulder bag, which presumably contained her firearm.

Will said, "Easy. We didn't mean to startle you."

She kept her bag close to her side as her gaze shot from Will to Thora and back again. "What are you doing in my house?"

"We saw blood on the porch." He nodded to the bandaged hand clutching her purse strap. "How bad are you hurt?"

"A few stitches, but I'll live."

"What happened?" He kept his voice low and nonthreatening. Elise could be volatile even on a good day.

She hesitated, then said, "I went after some bushes in the backyard a little too aggressively with a pair of clippers. I couldn't find my old pair and the new ones were a lot sharper than I thought. Sliced a couple of my fingers." She came into the room but didn't put down her bag. She also made sure she kept both of them in her line of sight. "So you saw blood on the porch. That explains why *you* entered my house but why is she here?"

"I'm his backup," Thora said.

Will turned in surprise but didn't contradict her.

She also kept her voice calm and neutral. "I apologize for barging in like this, but we really were concerned for your safety."

Elise looked almost amused. "You're his backup? After what happened to you?"

Despite Thora's measured tone, Will could detect a note of tension. "I'm fine. A little worse for the wear, but like you, I'll live."

The casual way she was able to discuss her ordeal amazed him, as did the ease with which she'd taken control of the conversation.

"I'm glad you're okay," Elise said. "But I still don't understand why either of you came to my house in the first place."

"I can only speak for myself," Thora said. "I came because of the conversation we had at the pub the night I was taken. Something you said has been bothering me."

Will scrutinized Elise's expression. He saw nothing but a flash of annoyance. "What did I say?"

"You asked if I thought James Ellis Ridgeway could have been responsible for the accident that killed my husband. I can't help wondering why something like that would even cross your mind.

It seems so out of the blue. You didn't know Michael. You barely even know me."

Elise shrugged, but her eyes had gone ice-cold. Her gaze darted to Will as if she sensed a trap. "It was an observation based on what I'd read about the Weatherman. Why would it bother you?"

"You know why," Will said. "We can't help wondering if someone put the idea in your head. Ridgeway himself, maybe."

Her eyes flashed angrily. "That's ridiculous. But baseless accusations seem to be your stock in trade these days. Maybe you should try doing some actual police work."

He didn't take her bait, but instead nodded toward the hallway. "Seems as though you're doing enough investigating for both of us. I saw the corkboard, the case files…the envelope from the Donaldson Correctional Facility."

Thora drew a quick breath. "Will, what are you talking about?"

Elise cut in before he could answer. "You went through my office? You violated my privacy on the thinnest of excuses just so you could paw through my things? That's a new low even for you."

"You're right," he conceded. "I shouldn't have taken it that far, but I did and now you and I need to talk about what I saw."

Her chin came up. "What I do on my own time is my business. I don't owe you any explanations."

"But you do," Will said. "If you're giving Logan Neville access to sealed files, that's very much my business and warrants at least a conversation. Where we have that conversation is up to you."

She looked as if she wanted to tell him exactly what he could do with those sealed files, but instead, she shrugged. "Fine. We'll talk. But alone."

Will turned to Thora. "Can you give us a minute?"

Thora lowered her voice to a near whisper. "She still hasn't answered my question."

"I'll make sure we get back to it," he said. "Let me talk to her."

Thora seemed to ponder her options, then nodded. "Okay. But this isn't over."

"Not by a long shot," he agreed. "I'll call you later." He walked with her into the foyer and held open the screen door.

She turned to him on the porch, her voice still a whisper. "Be careful, Will. There's something about the way she looks at you. Don't let your past with her cloud your judgment."

The way my past with you clouds my judgment? "You're the one I'm worried about," he said. "Go straight home, okay? No stops. No distractions. I'm texting Claire right now to expect you."

He waited on the porch until she was safely in the car before going back inside. The room was empty.

"Elise?"

"Back here."

He found her seated at the kitchen table with a bottle of whiskey and two empty glasses. She poured a generous dollop in her glass and hovered the bottle over his.

"No, thanks. It's a little early for me."

"For me, too, but I need something to take the edge off." She held up her bandaged hand. "Hurts like hell."

"Since when did you get so careless with your gardening tools?"

"Since I realized I could take out my frustrations on the shrubbery."

"Seems like the shrubbery has decided to fight back."

Pulling out a chair, he surreptitiously glanced around for her bag before he sat. He wondered if she'd found a strategic hiding place for her weapon while he'd been on the porch.

Her eyes glittered with emotion as she stared at him across the table. "We used to banter like this all the time, remember?"

"I do."

"We'd sit right here after work and have a drink, shoot the breeze until we decided what to do about dinner." She circled the rim of the glass with her finger. "Sometimes we'd forego dinner altogether."

"Elise."

"We were good together, Will. If only you'd

been able to let go of the past. And now you're bringing your past into my house."

"I didn't bring her here," he said. "I had no idea she was coming."

"You both just turned up here at the same time? Come on."

"I'm telling you the truth."

"Whatever." She poured another drink and downed it without flinching. "Let's get this over with. I've got things to do."

Will nodded and got right to the point. "Why are you investigating the Danny Hagan case off-book?"

"I'm no longer a CID detective, remember? I have to investigate off-book."

"Why Danny Hagan?"

"Because someone has to." She shoved her glass aside, but her gaze never left his. "I ran into his mother a few months ago. She remembered me. Came right up to me on the street and asked point-blank if anything was going on with her son's case. You have no idea how small I felt when I couldn't give her an answer. I told her I'd find out and get back to her. Turned out, nothing was being done. And that's on you."

"He disappeared ten years ago," Will said. "Do you know how many active cases we get in a month? Hell, in a week?"

"You sound defensive."

Yeah, maybe he was a little. "What did you

think you'd find that we couldn't when the trail was fresh?"

"Who knows? Technology changes every day. Circumstances change. Ten years ago, we'd never even heard of James Ellis Ridgeway, let alone that he started his serial killer career preying on children. The lead detective was convinced the stepfather did it and we let his tunnel vision rub off on us."

"Just because we couldn't prove it doesn't mean he didn't do it," Will said. "James Ellis Ridgeway is a long shot, unless you know something I don't."

She coiled a corkscrew curl around her finger. "What if I do? Know something you don't, that is."

"Care to share?"

She dipped her head as if afraid he might read the truth in her eyes. "Not yet. Not until I'm sure."

"Is that why you're trying to access sealed records?"

"Who says I am?"

"That's not a denial."

She leaned in. "What's the matter, Will? Are you worried I'll solve a case you couldn't?"

"It wasn't my case."

"Guess what, Deputy Chief? They're all your cases now. How will it look when a cop you had transferred out of Criminal Investigations solves a disappearance that has haunted this town for a decade?"

"Is that what this is about?" Will asked. "You trying to prove you're a better detective than I am?"

"Oh, honey. I've always been the better detective."

He knew she was trying to get a rise out of him, so he merely shrugged. "If you have it all figured out, why did you take the case to Neville?"

"Because I still have a full-time job. I needed help with research and legwork, and like it or not, he and his team have had success solving cold cases."

"The best I can tell, his team consists of a few overconfident students."

She sat back in her chair. "Look how dismissive you are, but you and I were once just like them. Remember how gung ho we were in the beginning before we got jaded? There's something to be said for that kind of naive zealotry."

"Zealotry?"

"Enthusiasm, if you prefer."

He toyed with his empty glass. "What's your current relationship with Logan Neville?"

"Why? Are you jealous?"

"I'm wondering what the two of you were arguing about on your front porch yesterday."

Her expression hardened. "That's personal and none of your business."

"Have you been in contact with James Ellis Ridgeway?"

"No comment."

"Did he tell you where to find the boy's remains?"

"No comment."

"Did he say anything about Thora Graham?"

"No. Comment."

He folded his arms on the table. "I have a theory."

Her tone turned bitter. "Oh, I'm sure you do."

"You went to the prison pretending to be Thora so that Ridgeway would agree to see you. He probably figured out the sham the moment he laid eyes on you. But he was willing to make a bargain anyway. He'd give you the location of Danny Hagan's remains if you arranged Thora's abduction. Am I getting warm?"

"Ice-cold, but I'm flattered you think I'm that devious. And capable. Kidnapping a woman with Thora's training and experience and burying her alive wouldn't be easy."

"You'd need help," Will agreed. "A partner in crime, so to speak. Maybe that's what you and Neville argued about yesterday. He's lying low and letting you take the heat."

She rose slowly and stood staring down at him. "You've always held a high opinion of your detective skills, one that I never shared. Now's the time to put up or shut up. If I'm the monster you seem to think I am, then all you have to do is prove it." She put her hands on the table and leaned toward him. *"Prove it."*

Chapter Fourteen

The neighbor's curtain twitched as Will strode up the walkway to Thora's townhouse late that afternoon. He waved at her and then went next door to ring the bell. He imagined Thora glancing out the peephole a split second before the dead bolt disengaged. She looked surprised when she drew back the door.

"Will! I wasn't expecting you in person." Her gaze narrowed. "Wait. Did Claire ask you to come over?"

"She did, but she's not the only reason I'm here. I wanted to touch base after my meeting with Elise."

"I wondered why I hadn't heard from you." She stepped back to allow him to enter. "What happened?" He followed her into the living room and she motioned to the sofa. "Can I get you something to drink before we talk? Claire made iced tea earlier. Or would you prefer something stronger?"

"If you have it."

"I don't have any beer, but I've got tequila for margaritas."

"Maybe not that strong. I need to keep a clear head."

"Wine it is, then." She left the room for a moment and came back with a bottle and two glasses. Settling on the sofa beside him, she poured the merlot and then tucked her legs beneath her. Will could smell lavender in her hair and on her clothes, but he couldn't be certain the scent was even real.

They sipped in silence until she set her glass on the coffee table and turned expectantly. "The suspense is killing me. What did Elise have to say?"

"She wouldn't admit to contacting Ridgeway, but I found an empty envelope in her desk with a Donaldson Correctional Facility return address. At some point, she must have written to him and he responded." He took another drink and then set aside his glass. "I asked if she'd gone to see him. I even went so far as to suggest she and Ridgeway had made a deal—the location of Danny Hagan's remains for your abduction."

Thora propped her elbow on the back of the sofa as she turned to face him. "What did she say to that?"

"She told me to prove it."

"But she didn't deny it."

"She didn't." He still had a difficult time accepting Elise's culpability, but worrisome things were starting to add up. "I didn't mention this earlier, but I was on campus before I saw you at Elise's house. I found something in your office."

"Why didn't you say anything?"

"We got sidetracked by the blood on the door and a few other things. I was hoping to find Logan Neville, but I decided to have a look around while I was there. Your door was unlocked. Is that usual for you?"

"No, I'm certain I locked it when I left on Friday."

"Anyone else have a key?"

She shrugged. "Any number of people including the custodial staff. It's the office reserved for temporary staff. People come and go."

"You keep a makeup bag in your bottom drawer," he said. "I found an auburn strand of hair caught in the zipper."

A frown flitted. "You think it's Elise's?"

"I don't know of any other redheads who'd have a reason for going through your belongings, do you?"

"No, but even if DNA could prove it was hers, a strand of hair is pretty flimsy evidence," she said. "Not as flimsy as a collection of Sherlock Holmes stories on her bookshelf, but as you said, not a smoking gun. What's the next step?"

"We still need to find Neville. His TA said he'd probably already left for his summer sabbatical. She claimed not to know his location. I'm wondering if he left town in a hurry so that Elise would have to take the heat for those sealed records. Or maybe he doesn't yet want to reveal why he's so anxious to get his hands on them."

"You think he's on to something?" An edge of excitement crept into her voice. "Maybe he found a connection to Ridgeway."

"That's one of several questions I'd like to ask him," Will said.

"You're the deputy chief. Can't you access sealed records? If we could take a look, maybe we could figure out what he found. Or what he suspects."

"It all depends on why the records were sealed," Will explained. "If opening the file could put someone's life in danger, for instance, we'd likely need a court order."

"How do you suppose Elise was able to gain access?"

"We don't know for certain that she did. Maybe Neville kept pressing her and she balked. Opening sealed files without proper authorization could be a career killer."

Thora leaned back against the sofa. "This is complicated."

"It is, but we're just getting started," Will reminded her. "The investigation is barely a day old and we've already uncovered quite a lot. We'll keep surveilling our suspects and investigating motives until we find our smoking gun. Criminals always make mistakes. We'll turn up the heat until someone breaks or screws up."

"In the meantime—"

He nodded. "In the meantime, you're left wondering if the person in the elevator with you is the one who kidnapped and buried you alive."

She picked up her glass and gulped wine. "Suddenly, I'm not feeling quite as safe in my home as I did a few minutes ago. Maybe I never really felt safe. New locks and security codes can only do so much."

Will rubbed the back of his neck where tension had set in. "I didn't mean to upset you."

"You can't worry about upsetting me," she said with blunt pragmatism. "You have a job to do."

"I could have been a little more tactful."

"It doesn't matter. Until we find the person or persons responsible, I'll be looking over my shoulder no matter what you say." Her chin came up. "But I refuse to cower in my house until he or she is caught. I haven't told Claire or my mom yet, but I'm going back to work tomorrow."

Will frowned. "You really think that's a good idea? Didn't the summer session just end? College campuses tend to be ghost towns between semesters."

"It won't be completely deserted," she said. "Most of us still have exams to grade and final scores to post. I also have student consultations all week and a meeting with the dean on Wednesday. It'll be a busy week. The sooner I reestablish a routine, the sooner I'll start to feel normal."

He wondered if she was as sure of herself as she seemed. "You'll call if you see or hear anything even the slightest bit troublesome or out of the ordinary?"

She nodded. "I won't take any chances, I promise."

They each picked up their glasses and sipped. The last thing Will wanted was to leave her alone, but he wondered if the reason she'd gone so quiet was her way of drawing their visit to a close. He set his glass down and rubbed a hand up and down his thigh.

"I should probably go—"

"I was just wondering—"

"You first," he said.

"Claire made a casserole for dinner. She happens to be a very good cook. If you don't have any plans—"

"I could eat," he said. "If it's not too much trouble."

"No trouble at all." She swung her legs off the sofa and stood. "I'll just go heat the oven."

He stood, too. "Anything I can do to help?"

They were face-to-face in close quarters between the sofa and the coffee table with no room to step aside. They dodged awkwardly for a moment until he put his hands on her shoulders.

The moment he touched her, something shifted

in her body language. Her eyes grew dark and heavy as she stared up at him. Then she took a quick step toward him. "Could I just—" She took his face in her hands and kissed him.

The feel of her lips against his was such a shock, he inadvertently drew away.

She looked embarrassed as she stumbled back. "I'm sorry. I didn't mean—"

"Hang on a minute. You caught me by surprise." He took a step toward her and slid his fingers through her hair as he tipped her face to his. He kissed her slowly and for a very long time. When he finally pulled away, he smoothed back her hair as he gazed into her eyes. "So it wasn't my imagination."

"What?"

"The lavender." He ran his fingers through the glossy strands. "I used to dream about that scent."

"You did?"

"Too many nights to count," he admitted.

"I dreamed about you, too." She hesitated, her eyes going dark with emotion. "For the longest time, those dreams made me feel guilty. I felt I was betraying Michael's memory."

That stung a little. "And now?"

"All I know is that those memories gave me something to cling to when I didn't know if I would see the light of day again. The sound of your voice kept me going. I know it sounds far-fetched, but in a way, you were there in the box with me."

"If I could have been there instead of you—"

"I know." She took his hand and drew it to her face, turning her lips into his palm.

His heart was starting to pound a little too hard for comfort. "I want to kiss you again, but I keep wondering if it's too soon. I don't want to rush you. I might scare you away."

"You're the only thing in my life right now that doesn't scare me. When I think about all those years without you…" She took a breath. "Thirteen years, Will. How did we let that happen?"

He touched his fingertip to her lips. "We need to talk about those thirteen years. There's a lot I need to say to you, but right now, tonight…"

She nodded, took his hand and wordlessly led him up the stairs.

A FAINT GLOW from the setting sun filtered into the bedroom through the gauzy curtains, making the encroaching twilight seem surreal and still far away. Will was already shirtless and shoeless. He walked over to close the blinds and for a moment, the absence of light alarmed Thora. She stood shivering in the center of the room until he moved back to her.

"Should I turn on a light?" he asked.

"No. Just…" She pulled his arms around her and kissed him.

He drew her T-shirt over her head, unfastened her bra and then she lay back on the bed while he tugged off her jeans. He shed the rest of his clothes and they crawled under the covers, familiar strangers, stroking and exploring. She ran her fingers over his shoulders and down his back, becoming reacquainted with the contours of his body. His hand slid up her leg, dipped to her inner thigh and she shuddered. It had been a long time since anyone had touched her so intimately.

"Will?"

He moved up beside her in bed until they were once again lying head-to-head on the pillows. They stared up at the ceiling as if they could already see the stars.

"It's been a long time for me," she said. "Is that a weird thing for me to tell you?"

"You can tell me anything." His voice was deep and impossibly intimate in the dimness of her bedroom.

She entwined her fingers with his as they lay side by side. "I've missed talking to you. There were so many times when I needed so badly just to hear your voice. You were my best friend. Sometimes I wonder what my life would have been like if I'd never left Belfort."

He turned to stare at her profile. "You've done important work since you left. You've been married and widowed. Those aren't small things. They made you the person you are today. If you'd stayed…who knows where we would have ended up? We were kids when we fell in love. We both needed to experience a bigger world. I don't fault you for leaving. But I'm glad you've finally come home."

She turned her head to meet his lips. One kiss became two and then suddenly they were both breathing heavily as he moved over her. His eyes were soft and mysterious as he gazed down at her. And then he smiled and Thora thought, *Now I'm home. I'm finally home.*

Chapter Fifteen

Thora spent all day Monday in her office grading finals. Her abduction had made the rounds and the curious glances from students and faculty that were left on campus were a bit off-putting but understandable. Some approached but most kept their distance, not really knowing what to say or how to act. She understood. How did one commiserate with a teacher or colleague who had been buried alive?

She tried to keep her head down and concentrate on work, but late that afternoon a general feeling of uneasiness invaded. People had been coming and going from the sixth floor for most of the day, but suddenly she became all too aware of the silence as the building emptied.

"Professor Graham?"

She jumped, her hand flying to her heart.

Baylee Fisher said contritely from the doorway, "I'm so sorry. I didn't mean to startle you. I was hoping to catch you before you left for the day. Do you have a minute?"

Thora glanced at her phone on the desk, took note of the time and motioned the young woman to the chair across from her. "What's on your mind?"

Baylee sat down, her gaze roaming the office curiously as she settled her messenger bag on her lap. She was a serious young woman with a tendency to self-isolate. Thora could sympathize. She'd turned into a bit of a loner herself these past few years.

"I hope this isn't a bad time." She looked anxious. "I know we don't have an appointment or anything, but I just wanted to stop by and tell you how glad I am that you're okay. And how much I admire the way you're handling everything that's happened. If I were in your place, I'd probably hide under the bed for a month."

Thora managed a smile. "A close, dark confinement is the last place I want to be."

"Yes. I can see how that would be." She tucked her short hair behind her ears as her gaze dropped to the phone on Thora's desk. "Did Deputy Chief Dresden mention our visit on Saturday?"

"What visit?"

"I went to the station after I heard you were missing. I told him that I'd overhead Professor Neville arguing with someone the day before. A woman, I think. They seemed quite angry, which is why I was so worried when I heard your name mentioned."

The hair at the back of Thora's neck prickled in alarm. "Mentioned how?"

"That's the thing. I don't know. I really couldn't hear the conversation. But now I'm wondering if the person with him was Elise Barrett. They were in a relationship a few months ago, but they had a falling out when he began showing too much attention to Addison."

"Do you mean Addison March?"

Baylee's eyes grew wide and solemn. "You do know the two of them are sleeping together, don't you?"

"I've heard rumors, but it's really none of my business," Thora said.

A frown flitted across her brow. "Oh, I know. I'm not the type to start gossip, but I just keep wondering why your name was mentioned in that argument—" She broke off as her gaze went to the window. "What's that noise?"

"I'm sorry?"

Baylee cocked her head as her voice lowered. "Don't you hear it?" She got up and moved to the window to stare out.

"Do you mean the flapping and clanging? It's the rope on the flagpole," Thora told her. "It does that all day if there's a breeze."

Baylee clutched her bag strap. "Doesn't it bother you?"

Thora glanced at her phone again, wondering when she could politely bring the conversation to a close. She was eager to get home, eager to get out of the building. "I'm used to it by now."

"I've heard that sound before." Baylee's voice was still low and now edged with dread. "There was a flagpole outside my bedroom window in one of the foster homes I was sent to."

"I didn't know you were in foster care," Thora said.

"No reason you should. I'm not looking for sympathy," she said. "Some of the homes were quite decent. The one with the flagpole outside my window though..." Her voice sounded distant, monotonous. Almost as if she'd put herself in some kind of trance as she thought back. "If the wind was up, the sound would keep me awake at night. I hated it at first until I realized all that flapping and clanging drowned out the footsteps."

"Footsteps?" A chill of apprehension stole over Thora.

"I used to hear them coming down the hallway, a sort of stealthy shuffling sound. They would pause at the room next door to mine. The girl in that room was a couple years older than me. Blonde, pretty, mature for her age. He would knock softly on the door with his fingertip—like this—so that he wouldn't wake up his wife or the other kids." She tapped on the windowsill as her gaze remained fixed on the flagpole. "I'd lie in bed listening to the ropes twist and flap in the wind so that I wouldn't have to hear that knock.

Or the sounds that came afterwards. Then one night he tapped on my door."

Baylee's voice had a mesmerizing quality as she unconsciously tapped her finger on the windowsill. Tap, tap…pause…tap, tap. Tap, tap…pause…tap, tap.

For a moment, Thora was so hypnotized by the girl's repetitive drumming that she missed the significance of the sequence. Then realization dawned as panic mushroomed in her throat. She swallowed back the fear and even managed a sympathetic smile as Baylee turned. But she must have glimpsed something in Thora's eyes or maybe she realized she'd inadvertently given herself away.

She said, "I shouldn't have done that. Maybe deep down in my subconscious, I wanted you to know."

Thora rose. "Know what?"

Baylee's hand slid inside her bag. Did she have a gun? A knife? Thora tried to calculate if she could reach her phone in time.

Baylee withdrew hedge clippers from the bag, the kind with long, pointed blades. An innocuous gardening tool that suddenly looked lethal.

"Don't try to pretend you don't know," she said. "It's beneath you. And don't bother screaming. Everyone has already left the building. I checked before I came to your office."

Thora was acutely aware of that phone just out of reach. "Why me?"

"Because of your connection to James Ellis Ridgeway. The plan wouldn't have worked otherwise. I'm sorry. You're my favorite professor. I know that I could have learned so much from you. But as much as I like and respect you, Elise Barrett despises you."

Thora shook her head in confusion. "You buried me alive for Elise Barrett?"

"*For* Elise? No."

"Then why?"

"It's simple, really. Professor Neville always used to say, if you want a perfect murder, you need a perfect patsy."

Images flashed through Thora's head as she rose. The auburn strand of hair carefully caught in her makeup bag. The volume of Sherlock Holmes stories placed on a top shelf in Elise's home where she likely wouldn't notice. The arguments with Logan Neville. Her bitterness over the breakup with Will. Her outrage at being transferred from Criminal Investigations. The lost garden clippers that were now undoubtedly in Baylee's clutches.

"Elise brought Danny Hagan's case to our team," she explained. "She was certain the Weatherman had abducted and murdered the child, and she wanted to be the hero detective who finally proved it."

"But Professor Neville had other ideas?" Thora asked.

"Oh, he was fully on board with the theory at first. But the deeper he dug, the more convinced he became that Danny had been lured away from the street and murdered by someone he knew, someone he looked up to, someone he trusted." Her eyes glinted dangerously. "He lived next door to my foster home. I was a bit older, and he looked up to me. When I suggested we ride our bikes out to the fire tower one day, he was beside himself with excitement. He always wanted to please me."

Thora eased toward the door. One on one, she might be able to hold her own, but Baylee had a weapon and the glassy eyes of the deranged. Better to avoid a physical confrontation if she could make a run for it instead.

"It was an accident," Baylee said as she tapped the clippers against her thigh. "He fell and bashed his head. I knew that I would be blamed and sent away from the only place that had ever seemed like a real home."

"So you hid the body."

"With a little help. And then I told the police I'd seen Danny get into his stepfather's truck that day."

"If you want the perfect murder…"

"Exactly. I knew that if Professor Neville got his hands on those sealed records, he would likely find my name on the witness list. I did everything

I could to make people think the Weatherman was calling the shots from prison through Elise Barrett. I even wrote letters to him and signed her name."

"Did you steal my ID so that you could visit him in person?"

"That actually was Elise. The woman is obsessed with proving her theory. That made her easy to manipulate."

Thora kept inching toward the door. "Why are you telling me all this?"

"Because I admire and respect you. You have a right to know why you were chosen. It wasn't personal. It wasn't at all your fault. It just had to be you."

The sound of Thora's ringtone startled them both. Baylee lunged for the phone on the desk as Thora whirled and dashed for the door. She sprinted down the hallway and was almost to the elevator when she realized she didn't hear pursuing footsteps. Was this all just a dream and she'd wake up back in the box?

The elevator doors slid open. She called out, "Help me!"

Addison March stepped out. She said in surprise, "Professor Graham! What's wrong?" Then her gaze darted past Thora to Baylee Fisher coming down the hall with the clippers. "What's going on?"

Baylee said, "She knows. Stop her!"

Addison simultaneously blocked the elevator and swung her heavy bag toward Thora's head. She dodged the blow, caught the strap and slung Addison aside. She hit the floor hard with a sputtered oath, still managing to trip Thora as she dove for the elevator. She scrambled inside the elevator and reached up to smash a button. The doors slid closed before Addison could wedge her arm between them.

DOWN, DOWN, DOWN Thora descended until the elevator bumped to a stop. She sprang to her feet, ready to sprint for the entrance. When the doors slid open, she stepped out, then glanced around in confusion. She wasn't on the ground floor. She must have pushed the basement button by mistake. She started to get back into the elevator but the down button on the second car was already lit. They were coming after her. She needed a place to hide until she could find another way out. She thought about the stairwell, but no. One of them would have that covered.

She sent the empty car back to the ground level hoping to buy some time. It was dark in the basement but not pitch black. Late afternoon light filtered in through a row of windows near the ceiling. She glanced around for a weapon or a way out. An accumulation of desks, chairs and other items that had been removed during the renovation had been stored against the back wall and forgotten. Various doors opened into other parts of the basement. Supply rooms, utility closets…

Within a matter of seconds, Thora had scouted several hiding places, but her gaze kept straying back to those windows. If she could find a ladder or drag a table over to the wall and stack a chair on top, she could unlock a window or break the glass, hoist herself through and find help.

She tried the supply closet. Lots of cleaning products, mops, buckets and buffers but no ladder that she could find. She hurried over to one of the wooden desks and dislodged it from the pile. By this time, she'd worked up a sweat. The desk was heavy and chips in the concrete floor kept snagging the legs. Finally, she had it in place and went back for a chair. Time was ticking. She glanced across the room toward the elevators. Did they know she was in the basement or would they assume she'd gotten off the elevator on the first floor? They would have to be careful how they hunted her. The Criminology Building might be deserted, but there would be students milling about the grounds, faculty hurrying toward the parking lot, custodial staff finishing up work for the day. All she had to do was buy herself some time—

She stopped struggling with the desk as a sound invaded the quiet of the basement. The vibrating buzz of a silenced phone. Not hers. She'd left hers behind when she fled. She cocked her head, lis-

tening. The sound was very faint. She followed
it through the maze of furniture until she found
a metal grate that covered what must have once
been a utility crawl space. The vibration came
from within. As she peered through the grate, she
could see a faint illumination. Then the buzzing
stopped, and the light went out.

Maybe the phone had dropped out of a work-
er's pocket while he crawled through the tunnel
to make repairs. A phone meant contact with the
outside world, with Will. The phone or the windows? She stood indecisively for a moment until
the clang of the elevator propelled her into action.
She hunkered down, opened the grate and peered
into nothing but darkness. Her heart started to
pound and her palms grew clammy. She could
feel the steel-like trap of inertia closing in on her
as she started to tremble.

Behind her the elevator pinged.

Move!

She dropped to all fours and eased into the
tunnel, closing the grate behind her. The elevator doors slid open as she moved deeper into the
darkness.

Directly in front of her, the phone started to vi-
brate once more. She thrust her hand in despera-
tion toward the lighted screen. Her fingers met
something cool and smooth. The phone was encased in heavy plastic, the kind used in construc-
tion zones to mitigate dust. In the dull glow from

the screen, she could make out a face, the features contorted by death and the thick sheet of plastic that also encased the body.

Logan Neville.

By this time, her heart was pounding so hard she felt lightheaded. She couldn't pass out now. She couldn't give into terror. She had to think. She had to hide. She had to be smarter than Baylee Fisher and Addison March. They were students. She had years of experience on them.

But so had Logan Neville...

As quietly as she could, she lifted herself over the body and pressed herself against the plastic. Then she held her breath, hoping the phone wouldn't ring again to give away her hiding place. Stealthy footsteps move around the basement. Then nothing but silence.

Thora waited. In the deep quiet, she heard the descent of the elevator as it was called back to the basement, the ping as the car stopped and then the doors slid open and closed. A moment later, the elevator ascended. Still, she waited, pressed against Logan Neville's dead body. She didn't want to think about that, but how could she not? He'd been killed because he'd dug too deeply. He'd figured it all out, a case that could have garnered the kind of coverage and attention he'd craved more than anything.

She let another few minutes go by before she eased from her hiding place. Maybe if she could find something in one of the storage closets to slice open the plastic, she could use Neville's phone to contact the police...

Too late she heard a sound behind her. Baylee had also been waiting. She struck Thora a glancing blow, but it was enough to knock her off balance. She stumbled backward, crashing into chairs as she grappled for a handhold even as she went all the way to the concrete floor.

Baylee was on her in a flash, pinning Thora's arms to her sides as she lifted Elise's clippers high above her head.

Thora freed a hand and went for the clippers. Over the sounds of the struggle and the ringing in her ears, she became aware of a descending elevator. She might be able to fight off Baylee, but she couldn't take on Addison, too.

Someone got off the elevator. A light came on and then a familiar voice commanded, "Drop your weapon!" When Baylee refused, Will said, "The building is surrounded and Addison March is upstairs right now spilling her guts, hoping to cut a deal. She ratted you out in the blink of an eye."

Baylee hesitated. "She wouldn't do that. Not after everything we've been through."

"But she did. She told us everything. How you were in foster care together. How you bribed her to help hide Danny Hagan's body. How you claimed it was an accident, but she saw you push him off the fire tower. Years went by and you went your separate ways only to end up at the same college as criminology majors. The truth might never have come out if Elise Barrett hadn't brought Danny's case to Professor Neville. You had to stop him from finding out the truth so you came up with an elaborate scheme involving the Weatherman. You even encouraged him to invite Noah Asher onto his podcast to cement the theory. But Neville wasn't buying it, was he? You had to get rid of him before he could look at the sealed files. He was intended for the second coffin—a little torture for doubting your abilities before his ultimate demise—but you had to abandon that plan once we found Thora. After Elise was arrested, you could then claim the glory of solving his murder. Like I said, she told us everything. It's over, Baylee. Get up slowly and back away."

Still, she hesitated, her gaze darting about the room looking for a way out. Then she rose and dropped the clippers to the floor. "I won't serve a day in prison. Not with my background."

"I wouldn't count on that," Will said. "Regardless, you can kiss a career in law enforcement goodbye."

She shrugged. "So what? I'll probably get a book contract out of this. I'll be a bigger deal than Professor Neville ever was. Just you wait and see."

By this time, a half dozen officers were exiting the elevators and clattering down the stairwell.

Baylee was cuffed and read her rights as Thora watched it all in disbelief.

Baylee stepped on the elevator and turned with a smile. "See you soon."

A chill feathered down Thora's backbone as she wrapped her arms around her middle. Will came over and placed his hand on her shoulder. "You okay?"

"I'm okay. How did you know where to find me?"

"We traced Logan Neville's phone. Sorry it took so long."

"No worries," Thora said as she leaned her head against his shoulder. "I knew you'd come."

"Always." He wrapped his arms around her and held on tight.

* * * * *

Get 3 FREE REWARDS!

We'll send you 2 FREE Books plus a FREE Mystery Gift.

FREE Value Over $20

Both the **Harlequin Intrigue®** and **Harlequin® Romantic Suspense** series feature compelling novels filled with heart-racing action-packed romance that will keep you on the edge of your seat.

YES! Please send me 2 FREE novels from the Harlequin Intrigue or Harlequin Romantic Suspense series and my FREE gift (gift is worth about $10 retail). After receiving them, if I don't wish to receive any more books, I can return the shipping statement marked "cancel." If I don't cancel, I will receive 6 brand-new Harlequin Intrigue Larger-Print books every month and be billed just $6.49 each in the U.S. or $6.99 each in Canada, a savings of at least 13% off the cover price, or 4 brand-new Harlequin Romantic Suspense books every month and be billed just $5.49 each in the U.S. or $6.24 each in Canada, a savings of at least 12% off the cover price. It's quite a bargain! Shipping and handling is just 50¢ per book in the U.S. and $1.25 per book in Canada.* I understand that accepting the 2 free books and gift places me under no obligation to buy anything. I can always return a shipment and cancel at any time by calling the number below. The free books and gift are mine to keep no matter what I decide.

Choose one: ☐ **Harlequin Intrigue Larger-Print** (199/399 BPA GRMX)   ☐ **Harlequin Romantic Suspense** (240/340 BPA GRMX)   ☐ **Or Try Both!** (199/399 & 240/340 BPA GRQD)

Name (please print)

Address   Apt. #

City   State/Province   Zip/Postal Code

Email: Please check this box ☐ if you would like to receive newsletters and promotional emails from Harlequin Enterprises ULC and its affiliates. You can unsubscribe anytime.

Mail to the **Harlequin Reader Service:**
IN U.S.A.: P.O. Box 1341, Buffalo, NY 14240-8531
IN CANADA: P.O. Box 603, Fort Erie, Ontario L2A 5X3

Want to try 2 free books from another series! Call 1-800-873-8635 or visit www.ReaderService.com.

*Terms and prices subject to change without notice. Prices do not include sales taxes, which will be charged (if applicable) based on your state or country of residence. Canadian residents will be charged applicable taxes. Offer not valid in Quebec. This offer is limited to one order per household. Books received may not be as shown. Not valid for current subscribers to the Harlequin Intrigue or Harlequin Romantic Suspense series. All orders subject to approval. Credit or debit balances in a customer's account(s) may be offset by any other outstanding balance owed by or to the customer. Please allow 4 to 6 weeks for delivery. Offer available while quantities last.

Your Privacy—Your information is being collected by Harlequin Enterprises ULC, operating as Harlequin Reader Service. For a complete summary of the information we collect, how we use this information and to whom it is disclosed, please visit our privacy notice located at corporate.harlequin.com/privacy-notice. From time to time we may also exchange your personal information with reputable third parties. If you wish to opt out of this sharing of your personal information, please visit readerservice.com/consumerchoice or call 1-800-873-8635. **Notice to California Residents**—Under California law, you have specific rights to control and access your data. For more information on these rights and how to exercise them, visit corporate.harlequin.com/california-privacy.

HIHRS23

Get 3 FREE REWARDS!

We'll send you 2 FREE Books plus a FREE Mystery Gift.

FREE
Value Over
$20

Both the **Harlequin® Desire** and **Harlequin Presents®** series feature compelling novels filled with passion, sensuality and intriguing scandals.

YES! Please send me 2 FREE novels from the Harlequin Desire or Harlequin Presents series and my FREE gift (gift is worth about $10 retail). After receiving them, if I don't wish to receive any more books, I can return the shipping statement marked "cancel." If I don't cancel, I will receive 6 brand-new Harlequin Presents Larger-Print books every month and be billed just $6.30 each in the U.S. or $6.49 each in Canada, a savings of at least 10% off the cover price, or 3 Harlequin Desire books (2-in-1 story editions) every month and be billed just $7.83 each in the U.S. or $8.43 each in Canada, a savings of at least 12% off the cover price. It's quite a bargain! Shipping and handling is just 50¢ per book in the U.S. and $1.25 per book in Canada.* I understand that accepting the 2 free books and gift places me under no obligation to buy anything. I can always return a shipment and cancel at any time by calling the number below. The free books and gift are mine to keep no matter what I decide.

Choose one: ☐ **Harlequin Desire**   ☐ **Harlequin**   ☐ **Or Try Both!**
(225/326 BPA GRNA)   **Presents**   (225/326 & 176/376
                               Larger-Print   BPA GRQP)
                               (176/376 BPA GRNA)

Name (please print)

Address   Apt. #

City   State/Province   Zip/Postal Code

Email: Please check this box ☐ if you would like to receive newsletters and promotional emails from Harlequin Enterprises ULC and its affiliates. You can unsubscribe anytime.

Mail to the **Harlequin Reader Service:**
IN U.S.A.: P.O. Box 1341, Buffalo, NY 14240-8531
IN CANADA: P.O. Box 603, Fort Erie, Ontario L2A 5X3

Want to try 2 free books from another series? Call 1-800-873-8635 or visit www.ReaderService.com.

HDHP23

THE NORA ROBERTS COLLECTION

40% OFF!

Get to the heart of happily-ever-after in these Nora Roberts classics! Immerse yourself in the beauty of love by picking up this incredible collection written by, legendary author, Nora Roberts!

YES! Please send me the **Nora Roberts Collection.** Each book in this collection is 40% off the retail price! There are a total of 4 shipments in this collection. The shipments are yours for the low, members-only discount price of $23.96 U.S./$31.16 CDN. each, plus $1.99 U.S./$4.99 CDN. for shipping and handling. If I do not cancel, I will continue to receive four books a month for three more months. I'll pay just $23.96 U.S./$31.16 CDN., plus $1.99 U.S./$4.99 CDN. for shipping and handling per shipment.* I can always return a shipment and cancel at any time.

☐ 274 2595   ☐ 474 2595

_____
Name (please print)

_____
Address   Apt. #

_____
City   State/Province   Zip/Postal Code

> **Mail to the Harlequin Reader Service:**
> **IN U.S.A.:** P.O. Box 1341, Buffalo, NY 14240-8531
> **IN CANADA:** P.O. Box 603, Fort Erie, Ontario L2A 5X3

NORA2022